ANGELS DON'T KNOCK!

ANGELS
DON'T KNOCK!

A Novel

Dan Yates

Covenant Communications, Inc.

Published by Covenant Communications, Inc.
American Fork, Utah

Printed in the United States of America
First Printing: June 1994

01 00 99 98 97 96 95   10 9 8 7 6 5 4 3 2

Library of Congress Cataloging-in-Publication Data

Yates, Dan, 1934-
      Angels don't knock : a novel / Dan Yates.
           p.   c.m.
      Summary: Because of a typographic error, a young school teacher finds herself
engaged to a successful psychologist while being courted by the ghost of the man
she was destined to love.
         ISBN 1-55503-711-9 : $7.95
         [1. Ghosts -- Fiction.]   I. Title.
PZ7. Y2127An   1994   94-22438
[Fic] -- dc20   CIP
                                         AC

CHAPTER ONE

Even as a child, Samantha loved the mountains. It was not surprising that she requested the party to be held at her Grandfather Collens' home near Payson, Arizona. June fifteenth, 1973, Samantha's fifth birthday, proved to be a delightfully pleasant summer day. Samantha's parents took her and a few of her friends to Payson early that afternoon.

It was a wonderful party with cake, ice cream, Grandma's special apple pie, outdoor games, and finally the hike along the north rim trail. Seven energetic children scampered through the woods feeding squirrels, imitating bird calls, chasing an occasional lizard, and just having fun. No one ever knew for sure how Samantha became separated from the party. Her absence was not discovered until they had rounded the last trail marker on the way back to the house. Anxiety turned quickly to panic as the seriousness of the problem became apparent. It was less than an hour until dark.

Grandmother Collens raced to the phone, calling first the sheriff and then every neighbor in the area. Within half an hour, ten experienced woodsmen made their way, on horseback, toward the north rim. Just as the sun was about to drift out of sight over the west mountain, they reached the edge of the trail.

Suddenly, there she was. Five-year-old Samantha, walking alone out of the forest. Her grandfather was the first to reach her. Leaping off the horse, he scooped her into his arms and held on like he would never let go again.

"It's okay, Grandad," she said. "The army man helped me find my way home."

* * * * *

This is just a bad dream, isn't it? I'm going to wake up any second now, right? Samantha stared in disbelief at the "Out of Order" sign hanging on the elevator door. Sliding the strap of her purse over one shoulder and juggling the stack of test papers from her fifth-grade class, she walked toward the stairs.

This is the third time this week I've had to climb these seven flights. If they don't make good on their promise of a new elevator soon, I'm moving. By the seventh floor, her lungs felt like they were ready to explode.

Fishing a ring of keys from her purse, she walked down the empty hall to apartment 707. *Wouldn't you know it,* she thought, greeted by the sound of her ringing telephone. *With my luck, they'll hang up just as I get there.* It took several tries to get the key in the lock, but at last she managed.

"Hello?" she answered, tossing her purse and papers on the overstuffed brown sofa in her living room. It was Bruce.

"Samantha, darling, you sound out of breath. Is everything all right?"

"Yes, Bruce," she puffed. "Everything's fine."

"I take it from the sound of your breathing the elevator was out of order again?"

"Now, that's what I call perception. I'll bet you never dated a woman with stronger legs than mine. What's going on, Bruce?"

"I have a surprise for you, darling. Something I feel will make you very happy. May I pick you up for dinner?"

Thoughts raced through Samantha's mind as she tried to find an excuse that would spare Bruce's feelings. It had been a rough day at school and she desperately wanted to be alone for the evening, just to unwind. After strong consideration, she decided on the truth.

"Would you be angry with me if I asked for a rain check? It's been one of those days."

"I've already made reservations at the Cactus Garden. You always enjoy eating there."

"I know," she sighed, "but I'm really out of it. I'd love to have dinner with you tomorrow night, though."

"You won't reconsider, then?"

"Think of it this way, Bruce. Some time to myself will guarantee I'll be in a better mood. Depending on what your surprise is all about, that could be to your advantage, you know."

"Very well, darling," he conceded with obvious disappointment. "Try to get some rest, and I'll call in the morning."

"Don't call before noon. You know me and my Saturday mornings. Thanks for thinking of me tonight, Bruce. It was a tempting offer, if I wasn't so tired." She said good night, hung up the phone, and started for the front door that she had left standing open.

Halfway there she suddenly paused and glanced around, overwhelmed by the feeling that she was not alone. This feeling was not unfamiliar to Samantha. She had experienced it often from the time she was a child. It had been especially noticeable the last three years, after moving to this apartment. Never before, however, had the feeling been so intense. Scanning the room thoroughly, she satisfied herself that no one was there. With a shrug, she walked the rest of the way to the door, where she closed and bolted it.

Moving to the kitchen, she opened the refrigerator and surveyed the shelves for something, anything, suitable for dinner. *Some trade-off,* she thought. *A microwave pizza for the Cactus Garden. At times I wonder about you, Samantha Allen.*

At that moment a cold chill ran through her like an electric shock as the feeling of someone else in the room returned. She broke into a sweat. Closing the refrigerator door, she searched every inch of her apartment. It was empty, but the feeling would not leave her. Picking up a magazine, she thumbed through the pages trying to get her mind onto something else. It didn't help. The walls began closing in on her. She felt trapped.

In desperation, she reached for the phone and quickly dialed Bruce's number. "Hello?" came the voice on the other end. "This is the Vincent residence."

"Hi, Bruce, it's me, Sam," she said, trying to maintain a steady voice. "Is that dinner offer still open for tonight?"

"Of course, darling," he answered excitedly. "Have you changed your mind?"

"How soon can you pick me up?"

"I can be there in half an hour, Samantha."

"Make it twenty minutes, and you won't have to bother coming up. I'll meet you at the front door. Like I said, the elevator's out of order again."

CHAPTER TWO

The beauty of the evening was breathtaking. A full moon had already appeared in the eastern sky, even though dusk was still several minutes away. Samantha waited near the entrance to the Anderson Apartment Building and enjoyed a cool breeze that gently ruffled her short blond hair. Staring at the moon, she marveled at how large it looked. It lacked the brilliant luster of a full moon in the darkness of night, making it appear almost unreal. A smile crossed her lips as she compared it to Bruce. Like the moon, he lacked the luster of many younger men she had dated in the past. Often, since she had been seeing Bruce, she had to stop and ask herself what it was about him that appealed to her. The answer was always the same. She felt comfortable with Bruce.

Unlike the girlfriends she grew up with, Samantha never enjoyed dating that much. It was not that she lacked the opportunity; her phone rang constantly with hopeful admirers. But she seldom dated the same man twice, and never the third time.

It was in her early teenage years when the feeling first started. By the time she reached twenty it had grown enormously. The feeling was not easily described, but it left her with the strong conviction that there would be one special man in her life. One man that destiny had chosen for her. Even though she didn't know how to recognize that man when he came along, she knew it would happen naturally. It was this haunting conviction that kept her from pursuing the friendship of most men she had dated. None of them answered the test.

Bruce was different. True, he was not the man she had searched a young lifetime for, but he was different. With Bruce she felt comfortable, perhaps because of their age difference. He was eight years her senior. Then again, she might have been attracted to Bruce because he never really grew up. He remained a perpetual boy. Being a school teacher, Samantha often thought of him as one of her students, only larger. Helping him become a better man presented an intriguing challenge she felt compelled to accept.

Bruce already had his good points. He always treated her with gentle respect, and at times could be very romantic.

She and Bruce had been seeing each other for about six months, and she had grown quite fond of him. She had even begun to doubt the reality of her other feelings. Perhaps her knight in shining armor was nothing more than a childish fantasy, like believing in Santa Claus. On the other hand, with a lot of work she might be able to mold Bruce into that knight in shining armor.

Just then, a familiar black Lexus pulled up to the curb directly in front of her.

"Thank goodness you're ready," Bruce said as she slid into the seat next to him. "I hate leaving my car unattended in this neighborhood."

"I don't know why you make such a big thing out of my neighborhood, Bruce. No one's bothered your precious car yet, have they?"

"No, but I've increased my theft insurance, at no small cost mind you, since I've been parking it here."

"Why not leave it at home and take a taxi? Better yet, do as I do and ride a city bus."

"Where would you like to eat, darling?" he asked, ignoring her remark. "I canceled my earlier reservations. You didn't give me much time to make new ones, you know."

"Let's go to McDonald's for a Big Mac and fries."

"Samantha! You know my feelings about fast-food houses. Now seriously, where would you like to eat?"

"You know what you are?" she asked, giving him a gentle shove to the shoulder. "You're a stuffy person who has no idea how to have fun. I'm going to teach you how to enjoy life if it's the last thing I do." She noticed that his left eye had begun to twitch. It always twitched when something was bothering him.

"We'll eat at the Hunter's Cottage," he responded indignantly. "I can always get a table there on short notice."

Bruce tipped the valet, and the two entered the rustic building just as night had begun to fall.

Inside, Samantha found her appetite quickened by the tantalizing aroma from the kitchen. A lively little man at the organ played a delightful version of a song that stirred her memory.

In the lobby, a large group of people waited for tables. Bruce ignored them and walked straight to a man in a dark suit at the reception counter. Samantha watched as he handed something to the man. They were seated immediately at a secluded lakeside table on the outside patio.

As they settled into their seats, a young woman in a black skirt and white apron approached the table. "Would you like something to drink before your meal?" she asked.

"I'll have a Sprite," Samantha answered.

"A Sprite?" the young woman asked, a hint of scorn showing through her grin.

"If you don't have Sprite, any soft drink will do."

"I think we may have 7-Up."

"That'll do nicely, thank you."

"Make it two 7-Ups," Bruce quickly added, obviously embarrassed.

"Cool it, Bruce," Samantha whispered as the waitress walked away. "You ought to know by now—I'm a soft drink kind of person."

"It's all right," he smiled. "I suppose I wouldn't want you any other way. Perhaps I'll consider changing a few of my own bad habits, if that will please you."

"That's your decision, Bruce."

Bruce lowered the menu he had been reading. "Speaking of change, what made you reconsider having dinner with me tonight?"

"Why do you ask?"

"I know you pretty well, Samantha. Well enough to know that your first refusal was serious. Then, fifteen minutes later you changed your mind. That's just not you."

The waiter approached their table. "Are you ready to order, sir, or would you like a little more time?"

"I think we're ready."

"May I suggest the white crab? I think you'll find it simply superb."

"Is that all right with you, darling?"

"I'll have a steak."

Folding the menu, Bruce returned it to the waiter. "Two filets, medium well."

"Very well, sir. I'm sure you'll find our steaks to your liking. Would you care for soup or salad?"

"Two salads."

"I recommend our Italian dressing."

"I'll have the ranch," Samantha smiled warmly.

"I'm terribly sorry, madam," the waiter replied coldly. "We don't serve ranch dressing here."

"No ranch? Well," she sighed, "I guess I'll settle for blue cheese."

"Blue cheese it is. And you, sir?"

"I'll go with your recommendation."

"The Italian, very good choice indeed."

"By the way," Samantha said to the waiter, with a deliberate sparkle in her voice. "I prefer my filet butterflied. You do know how to do that here, do you not?"

"Of course," came the curt reply.

Bruce cleared his throat. "Butterfly the lady's, but I'll have mine just the way your chef specializes it."

The waiter left for the kitchen just as the young woman in the black skirt returned with the drinks.

"You didn't answer my question, darling."

"I changed my mind. So what's the big deal?"

"There's more to it than that; now let's have it. What's bothering you?"

"I had a hard day," she answered after taking a sip of 7-Up.

"You could give up all those hard days just by saying one word."

"Why can't they give you two straws with your drink? It always tastes better that way for some reason."

"You know I'm crazy about you."

"I know."

The waiter returned with the salads. Bruce studied Samantha closely until he was gone again. "Something's bothering you tonight. It's written all over your face."

"I can't help it, Bruce. I just like my soda better with two straws."

"It won't work this time. I refuse to let you joke your way out of this one. Tell me what it is that has you bothered."

"Isn't it enough for you to be a psychologist during office hours? Do you have to psychoanalyze your date as well?"

"It is my profession."

Samantha longed to talk, but didn't know how to approach the problem. How could she explain the strange feeling of someone being in her apartment, when she knew no one was there? She glanced at Bruce, who was staring hard at her. "You think you're smart, don't you?"

Bruce answered with a condescending smirk that she had learned to hate. Yet, right now she needed his help, so with a deep sigh, she spoke. "There is one little thing I might like to get your opinion on," she said nonchalantly, looking down at the bite of salad she had on her fork.

"Ah!" he exclaimed. "Now we're getting somewhere." Reaching across the table, he gave her hand a squeeze. "That's my girl. Now tell me the problem."

Samantha looked around to be sure no one else was near. "Well, Bruce, it's—hard to explain."

"Just say it, my darling."

"It's, well, it's one of my students." She hadn't intended to lie; the words just slipped out. "It's little Oscar."

"What about Oscar?"

"He, or rather his mother . . . well, something strange happened to her." Looking straight at Bruce, she asked the question outright. "Do you ever counsel clients who think they're being watched in their own home, when no one is actually there?"

"Of course. I handle that sort of thing every day. It's a common occurrence. Is that what happened to Oscar's mother?"

"Yes. What do you think causes that kind of thing to happen?"

"It's nothing serious. It's only a trick the mind plays on a person once in a while. It usually goes away in a day or two."

"It's lasted a long time with Oscar's mother. Each time it happens, it gets a little stronger. In fact, the last time it happened she felt it so strongly she had to leave the house to escape it."

Bruce released her hand and gave it a couple of pats. "Sounds to me like little Oscar's mother has been hitting the 'sauce' too hard."

"Bruce Vincent! Stop teasing me this instant! Oscar's mother doesn't drink. I was hoping for a serious answer from you."

"I only meant to. . ."

"Let it go," she snapped. "I'm not in the mood for this. I wanted your help, and you made fun of me."

"I don't understand, darling. Why are you so upset about something that happened to the mother of your student?"

"Eat your salad, Bruce." Her voice was icy cold. He obviously sensed a deeper problem but, for once, was wise enough to know when to back away. He ate his salad.

"Samantha, darling," he said after several minutes of silence, "I've been waiting for the right moment to bring something up."

Taking another sip of 7-Up, she studied his expression. She was sure what was coming had something to do with his constant pressure to set a marriage date. "Well?" she asked, a mild chill still in her voice. "Is there anything wrong with this particular moment?"

He removed a small black velvet box from his suit pocket. "I've taken the liberty of assuming that your answer, when it comes, will be 'yes.'"

She watched intently as he opened the box, revealing the most stunningly beautiful diamond ring she had ever seen. "What are you doing?" she gasped.

"I'm not asking for an exact date, you understand. I'm only asking you to wear my ring, as a promise that your answer will come soon."

"Bruce, I. . ."

"Please darling, you can't possibly know how important this is to me."

"Well, it is beautiful."

"And so are you, Samantha."

"I still need more time to. . ."

"I understand," he said, reaching for her hand and gently slipping the ring on her finger. "I promise to be patient, even though patience is not one of my stronger virtues."

Samantha studied the ring. It was stunning, set with nine stones—five diamonds and four sapphires. The diamond in the center was huge. "Bruce," she protested, "this must have cost you. . ."

He put two fingers gently against her lips. "The price is not important, darling."

She was not ready to marry Bruce just yet. She was certain, though, that she would decide to before too much longer. "It is gorgeous," she said at length.

"Then you will wear it?"

"All right, Bruce. I'll wear your ring."

"The butterfly for you, madam," the waiter said, having slipped unnoticed to their table. "For you, sir, the chef's special."

Samantha leaned back, staring at the steak. "Would you look at the size of that!" she exclaimed. "I'll never be able to eat it all."

"You've just made me the happiest man alive," Bruce beamed as the waiter walked away.

"Calling this a big steak made you the happiest man alive?"

"Samantha, stop that! You always have to make jokes when I'm trying to be serious. You know what I meant."

Samantha smiled affectionately at Bruce, while studying his face carefully. Looking past the overgrown boy, she saw what he could become and liked what she saw. She felt warm and secure with him nearby. The feelings she had earlier in her apartment seemed distant now. She was glad she had chosen to wear his ring.

CHAPTER THREE

Using Samantha's key, Bruce unlocked the door to her apartment. She stepped inside. He returned her keys and remained in the hall.

"That's not much of an elevator even when it's working, is it?" he scoffed.

"Don't knock it," she laughed. "When you've climbed those stairs as often as I have, you won't be so picky about the elevator."

Slipping his arms around her, he leaned in and kissed her cheek. "Oh, Samantha, I love you so. Why won't you let me take you out of all this? Just say the word, and you'll never have to climb those stairs again."

"Bruce, you promised. . ."

"To be patient, I know, but it's so hard leaving you here. This place gives me the creeps."

"You worry too much. What mugger, in his right mind, would climb seven flights of stairs to rob a fifth-grade schoolteacher?"

"You make jokes, but it's my job to keep you safe."

"You think of me as a job? I'll tell you what. Either you get out of here and let me get some sleep, or you're fired, okay?"

He took a deep breath. "May I call you tomorrow?"

"Not before noon!"

"Good night, darling," he said reluctantly, kissing her lightly on the lips.

"Good night, Bruce. Thanks for dinner, it was terrific. I'll wear your beautiful ring, and I promise to think about setting a date." She watched as he crossed to the elevator and pressed the call button. Nothing happened. He pressed it again, with the same results.

"Either you marry me soon," he grumbled on his way to the staircase, "or you get an apartment on the ground floor. I can't take much more of this physical fitness thing every time I come up here."

She smiled at his grumbling and watched until he was out of sight, then closed and secured her door.

Once inside, she paused to see if the feeling was still there. It seemed to have left her, but she looked over the apartment just the same. To her left was the small kitchen and dining area with its table and two chairs. No one there.

Directly in front of her was the living room. It was unoccupied as well.

She cautiously crossed to the bedroom, leaving her purse and keys atop the sofa table on the way. She peered inside; the bedroom was empty.

Breathing a sigh of relief, she decided on a relaxing shower before bed. Then suddenly the feeling returned. It was even stronger than before. Out of the corner of her eye, she caught a glimpse of something. Whirling around, she saw him.

"What are you doing in my apartment?!" she screamed. It was a man, standing just inside her front door.

"Take it easy, Sam," the intruder said with a calming hand gesture. "I know seeing me this way is a shock. Believe me, I'm not here to harm you in any way."

"I've got a gun!" she yelled. Dashing to the bedroom closet, she frantically rummaged through the items on the upper shelf. The intruder remained motionless, watching her through the open bedroom door. Eventually, she produced an old revolver. "I'm not afraid to use this!" she shouted, pointing the weapon directly at him.

"Put that thing down, Sam, before you hurt yourself!"

"I'm not kidding, I'll . . . wait a minute! How do you know my name?"

"I'd be glad to tell you if you'll put that useless, rusty thing away."

"It's not useless! I use it all the time! Get out of here this instant, or you'll find out how well it works!"

"We both know you've never fired a weapon in your life, Sam."

"That's a lie. I'm an excellent shot."

"Well then, go ahead—make my day."

"Get out!" she cried, waving the revolver wildly.

"Sam, that gun was useless when your Grandfather Collens gave it to you five years ago."

She walked to the door, taking one step into the living room. "How do you know my grandfather's name?"

"He told me."

"You knew my grandfather?"

"I still know him."

Squeezing the gun so tightly her fingers grew numb, she glared at the intruder. "You're a liar!" she spit out. "My grandad is dead."

"I know that. He and your grandmother were killed a year ago in a car accident. I was there when it happened."

"What is this?!" she demanded. "How do you know these things?"

"Sam, please calm down. Do I look the least bit dangerous? Aren't you even a little curious about me? Wouldn't you like to know who I am, and why I'm here?"

"No!" she snapped. "I have a boyfriend! If you hurt me, you'll have to answer to him!"

"You can forget about Bruce. I'm not going to hurt you, Sam."

"I don't believe this!" she screamed. "You even know about Bruce?"

"Of course I know about Bruce. He's in the parking lot right now, checking to see if his precious car is all right. I'd hate to think you had to depend on that wimp for protection."

"Get out!" she exploded as fury began to supplant her fear.

He crossed his arms and stared hard at her. "No, Sam," he said. "I don't want to frighten you, but I've waited over twenty years for this moment. I'm not about to let it slip away from me now."

Her mind whirled in confusion at this remark. "What moment?" she barked.

"The moment," he answered softly, "when I would no longer have to remain in the shadows of your life, but could finally reveal myself to you."

"Who are you?" she demanded in a voice so shrill, it even shocked her.

"Jason."

"What?"

"You asked who I am. I'm Jason Hackett," he said. Then she watched with a startled expression as he walked leisurely to her sofa and took a seat.

"What do you want from me?" she asked, still pointing the old revolver at him.

"Take it easy, Sam," he pleaded. "I only want to talk. I give you my word, you have nothing to fear."

She stared at him intently. He remained frozen in place, as if giving her time to evaluate the situation.

"Where did you come from?" she blasted. "I know you weren't there when I came in from the hall."

"You're right, I wasn't. I followed you in."

"That's impossible. The door's locked, and the chain secured." She gave a quick look at the door to be sure. It was just as she had left it.

"Well, you see, Sam," he said, with a bit of a shrug, "in my present state, locked doors don't mean much."

"How can you get through a locked door?"

He broke into a laugh. "I'm not sure that you're ready to hear how."

"I want you to leave, now!"

He laid a hand to his forehead and breathed a sigh. "I know how hard this is for you, but I just can't leave yet. We have to talk sometime, and it won't do either of us any good to put it off."

"That's absurd. Why should I ever have to talk to you?"

He leaned back on the sofa and studied her closely. "You know what I think? I think you're beautiful."

Caught completely off guard by his remark, she couldn't manage an answer. Her mouth fell open and she stood motionless, staring at him. Without thinking, she lowered her hand and let the revolver drop to the floor.

"There's no reason to be afraid of me, you know. I couldn't hurt you, even if I wanted to."

He held up one hand and looked at it, slowly turning it from one side to the other. "Does this look like a regular old hand to you, Sam? Well it's not. Do you know what would happen if you tried to shake this hand? It would be sort of like trying to hold a dream. When you reached for it, nothing would be there."

"A dream," she stuttered. "Yes, that must be it. You're only a dream. Bruce brought me home, I had a hot shower and went to bed.

I must have eaten too much steak."

"Sorry, Sam," he said, slowly shaking his head. "You're not dreaming. You've never been more awake in your life."

Her mind raced in thought. *You're right, this is too real to be a dream. How else can this all be explained? Unless* . . . "Good grief!" she cried. "Are you a ghost?!"

"I'm not a ghost!" he yelled, leaping to his feet. "I hate being called that! Ghosts are creatures that go around haunting and frightening people."

"Well, what do you think you're doing to me right now?!"

"Oh," he said, quickly falling back to the sofa with a sheepish look on his face. "I—I'm sorry. I just got carried away when you called me that."

"If you think you're not frightening me, I'd like to know what you'd call it."

"I said I was sorry. I don't want to frighten you. I had to find some way of meeting you, and this was the best I could come up with."

"What do you mean you had to meet me, and how did you get in my apartment with the door locked?"

"I've been trying to explain. Locked doors can't keep me out."

"Are you trying to tell me," she stammered, "that you can . . . ?"

"Walk through walls?"

"I can't believe I'm having this conversation!"

"Yes, I can walk through walls, or locked doors, or whatever you want me to walk through."

"This is insane! There's no such thing as a ghost. There's no such thing as someone who can walk through walls, either. There has to be another explanation."

"Okay, you tell me how I got in here, then."

"I don't know, but you didn't walk through a wall."

"Look, I'll prove it to you," he said, standing up.

"What are you doing? Don't come near me!"

"Why do you have to be so hard to get along with? If you want proof, you have to let me get to the wall first."

She watched intently as he moved to the wall next to the hall door. Her fear of this intruder was rapidly turning to anger.

"Look!" she snapped. "I'm not sure what this little game is all about, or how you got in my apartment, but we're going to have to come to some kind of an understanding. You can't just pop in on me like this. I want you out of here, do you understand?"

"I'll go halfway with you, Sam. I'll walk out, just to prove I can do it. But afterwards, I'm coming right back in. I still have to talk to you."

"Do you really expect me to believe you can walk through that wall?"

Jason turned on his warmest smile. "I'll make you a deal, Sam. If I can't walk through the wall, I give you my word I'll walk out your door and never return. On the other hand, if I do walk through the wall, I want your word you'll listen to my story. Is that fair?"

Slowly she made her way to the sofa, where she was within reach of the phone. She didn't pick it up, but wanted to be close to it just in case. "You want me to listen to your story?" she asked, never taking her eyes off him.

"That's why I'm here in the first place, to get you to listen to my story."

"Why in the world would you want that?"

"I know you don't realize it, lady, but you happen to hold the key to my whole future. If I can't convince you to listen to my story, I'm in deep trouble."

"This conversation gets crazier by the minute."

"What about my offer?" he pressed. "Is it a deal, or not?"

She hesitated before answering. "Let's make sure we understand each other. If you can't do it, you have to leave and never come back, right?"

"Agreed. And when I do walk through the wall, you have to listen to my story, okay?"

"Do I have your word you'll leave?"

"You do, if I have your word on your part."

"Okay, you have my word. But don't expect me to seal it with a handshake."

"Fair enough," he chuckled. "Shall I get on with it?"

"Be my guest," she said, folding her arms tightly.

"Maybe it would be better if you sit down first."

"Oh, I see. Here comes the stall, right?"

"Please, Sam, sit down. I really think it would be better."

She slowly slipped to the sofa, watching him closely all the while. "There, I'm sitting down. What's your next excuse?"

"I don't have one," he said, smiling mischievously. "Let's do it." Slowly and deliberately he turned to the wall. Then, with no hesitation, he stepped directly into it.

CHAPTER FOUR

"Oh, no," she moaned. "Not the phone. Not this early." Through half-open eyes she watched the white blob on the nightstand gradually take the shape of an extension phone. By the fourth ring she managed to answer a half-hearted, "Hello?"

"Darling, it's me, Bruce."

"Why am I not surprised? You promised not to call before. . . "

"I know I promised, but I was worried."

"Why can't you learn to worry about me at a decent hour?"

"Are you still wearing my ring?"

"Of course I'm still wearing it," she said, sliding up on the edge of the bed. "Is that why you called, to see if I had run away with another man?" Something on the floor next to the bed caught her attention. She looked more closely to discover it was the clothes she had worn yesterday, lying in a wadded pile on the floor. *I must have really been out of it last night,* she thought. *I never treat my clothes that way.*

"Darling, don't be ridiculous. I was worried because you were acting strangely last night."

"What do you mean, I was acting strange last . . . ? Oh!" she gasped, suddenly remembering.

"What is it, darling? Did something startle you?"

"No, nothing like that. I just remembered a strange dream I had last night."

"What sort of dream?"

"I don't know, something about a ghost in my room."

"A ghost? How amusing," he chuckled.

"Stop laughing at me, Bruce! You know how I hate it when you do that."

"I wasn't laughing at you. I was laughing at your crazy dream.

May I see you tonight?"

"I don't know, I'm not even awake yet. Call me back at a reasonable hour."

"What would be a good time?"

"You figure it out, but if it's before noon I promise to kill you."

"I'll call about one-thirty."

"Goodbye, Bruce, I'm hanging up now." Without waiting for his reply, she shoved the phone back on the hook and buried her face in the pillow. "What a weird dream," she mumbled.

"Wasn't a dream, Sam."

"What?" she cried, tossing the pillow aside. "Oh no, tell me it's not true! You really were here?"

"I still am. I never left."

"You're in my bedroom!" she shrieked, pulling the sheet tightly around herself. "Get out of here, or I'll scream so loud everyone in the building will hear."

"I'm going." His hasty retreat to the living room might have been humorous under other circumstances.

"Shut the door!" she yelled. He didn't answer.

After assuring herself he was out of sight, she grabbed a robe from the closet and hurriedly threw it on. Easing to the door, she peered into the living room. He was there, with his back toward her.

"I asked you to shut the door. Why did you ignore me?"

"I can't shut the door, Sam. I explained that last night."

"Oh, that's right. I forgot you're a . . . what happened last night, anyway?"

"You fainted."

"I what?"

"You fainted."

"How did I get to bed? You didn't . . . ?"

"No, Sam, I didn't."

"Then how did I get to bed?"

"You came to your senses long enough to stagger in there yourself."

"You do know I could call 911 and have you arrested, don't you?"

"Sam, I've told you, I mean no harm. But if you want to call, there's no way I can stop you."

"Why are you still here? You made a deal with me to leave. Does your word mean nothing to you?"

"May I turn around?"

"I suppose so. But don't come near me!"

"Our deal was, I would leave if I couldn't walk through that wall."

Adjusting the collar of her robe, she struggled to remember what had happened last night. She recalled he had turned to the wall; after that—nothing. "Are you trying to tell me," she asked, "that you did walk through a wall?"

"That's right."

"Do you lie about other things, too?"

"Oh," he said, just now turning around, "you think I'm lying. Well, would you mind explaining why you fainted?"

"Are you absolutely sure I fainted?"

"I'm positive."

"Then you must have done something to frighten me."

"That's exactly what I did. I walked through that wall, right over there."

"Okay, there's a simple way to settle this. If you walked through a wall last night, as you claim, do it again right now and I'll be convinced."

"Sorry, Sam, no deal."

"See?" she said, folding her arms. "I rest my case. You can't do it."

"I can if I want to, but you don't seem to handle it well when I do."

I have to know, she thought to herself. *Something happened last night, but what? What caused me to faint?* Then an idea came to her.

"That's it!" she cried, rushing back into the bedroom. "I'm calling 911." Lifting the receiver, she pretended to make the call, watching out of the corner of her eye to see what he would do.

She had caught him completely off guard. He followed her as far as the doorway to see what she was up to. This was exactly what she wanted him to do.

If Mohammed won't go to the wall, she figured, *why not take the wall to Mohammed.* Grabbing the pillow from her bed, she hurled it at him as hard as she could.

At that moment, everything seemed to shift into slow motion. She watched the pillow fly toward him. He made no effort to move, nor did he make an effort to block it. The pillow passed completely through him and landed on the floor next to the sofa. Her eyes widened, her mouth fell open, and she felt her knees go weak.

"Please!" he shouted, with an outstretched hand. "Don't pass out again!"

"I don't believe it!" she cried. "You really are a ghost!"

"No, Sam! I told you I'm not a ghost!"

"Why are you haunting me? What did I do to deserve this?"

"Sam, why can't you understand that I'm not haunting you?"

She fell to a sitting position on the edge of the bed and stared hard at him. "If you're not haunting me," she asked at length, "exactly what is it you are doing?"

"I'm, well, I'm sort of. . . "

"You're sort of what?" she demanded.

"Sort of. . ." He shrugged, and his face twisted into a foolish grin. "Sort of courting you, I guess."

"What!" she shrieked. "Are you insane?"

"Well, I suppose courting's not the best word for it, but it's as close as I can come at the moment."

"I'm being courted by a ghost?"

"Sam, please stop calling me a ghost. I hate it when you do that."

"Enough!" she shouted, shaking her finger at him. "Get out of my apartment—this instant!"

"I can't! Not until you've listened to my story."

Springing to her feet, she pointed in the direction of the hall door. "I said get out! Now go!"

"Are you forgetting our agreement, or does your word mean nothing to you?"

She grew quiet. Her hand dropped to her side. "How dare you," she asked in a subdued voice, "use my own words against me?"

"If the pillow thing's not good enough to convince you, I'll walk through your blasted wall. Any way you look at it, though, you lost. You owe it to me to listen to my story."

"All right," she quietly conceded. "I'll keep my word, but I need a little breathing room. It's not every day a woman finds herself confronted by a gho . . . well, whatever you are."

"I'm just Jason. Nothing more, nothing less."

"Look, we need to set one ground rule right now. You keep your distance. Don't even think about coming near me."

"How about giving me a little credit? Have I tried to get close to you yet?"

"No, I suppose you haven't."

"You have my word. I'll respect your ground rule."

"All right, I'll listen to your story. But I would like to get dressed first. Is that asking too much?"

"Be my guest, but you'll have to close your own door."

"I'll close the door after you back away from it."

"I'm gone." He laughed and walked to the far side of the living room, next to the fake fireplace.

About ten minutes passed before Sam came out of the bedroom wearing a pair of blue jeans and a white sweater.

"Wow!" he said. "Don't you look sharp!"

"I thought you were supposed to be dead," she replied, walking to the sofa.

"Hey! I'm not that dead."

"Look, I agreed to listen to your story, not to have you make passes at me."

"I'm not making a pass at you. I just like the way you look in those jeans, that's all."

She dropped to the sofa. "If you want to tell me your story, then get on with it. Otherwise, you can leave."

"Take it easy, Sam. There's so much to tell it's hard to know where to start."

"Why not start at the beginning? That usually works well."

He laughed. "I'm aware of that. It's just hard to know where the beginning of my story really is. Maybe a good place to start would be the year 1968."

"That's the year I was born."

"I know, Sam, and that has a lot to do with my story." He turned toward the fireplace and spent several moments in thought. "There's something I want you to know before we go any further."

"And that is?"

"I want you to know I would never do anything to hurt you, in any way."

"Oh sure," she smirked, "and I'm supposed to trust you, just like that?"

"Watch this," he said, moving to the mantel over the fireplace where she kept a photograph of Bruce. He reached for the photograph as if to pick it up. She watched in amazement as his hand simply passed through the picture without moving it at all. Again and again he tried to lift the picture, each time with the same result.

"You see, I couldn't hurt you even if I wanted to." He turned to face her once more. "I tell you with all my heart, Sam. I would never want to."

"You make a good argument, but keep your distance anyway. I just feel better about it, okay?"

"I'll keep my distance," he sighed.

She noticed a sadness in his eyes, but only for a moment, then he smiled at her. Thoughts flooded her mind. Was she really talking to a ghost, or was she still asleep? If she was awake, was she imagining the whole thing? Whatever was happening, her natural curiosity had been aroused. "May I ask you a personal question?"

"Of course, Sam."

"You won't get upset?"

"Why would I get upset?"

"Well it certainly seems to upset you when I call you a ghost."

"That's different. What's your question?"

"I saw the pillow pass through you, and you demonstrated you couldn't pick up the picture. I'm confused. How are you standing on the floor? Why don't you sink through it?"

"Good question," he laughed. "I had trouble with that one myself at first. After some practice I learned I could sort of float and give the appearance of standing on the floor. I can even sit down using the same method. I'm so used to it now, it's second nature. Look, I'll show you what I mean."

She watched in bewilderment as he drifted upward about two feet off the floor and levitated there.

"All right, I get the picture," she said motioning him back down. "I'd just as soon you stayed on the floor."

"Any more questions?" he grinned.

Leaning back on the sofa, she crossed her legs and folded her arms. "Let's hear your story," she said, for the first time showing a hint of a smile.

"I've waited over twenty years for this. Now I get the chance, and I can't believe how hard it is. I suppose it would be better to start further back than 1968." He drew a deep breath and let it out slowly. "Well, here goes nothing. Most stories begin with 'once upon a time.' Not mine. Mine has to start with 'once upon a typo.'"

"Once upon a what?"

"A typo."

"I don't understand."

"Everything was going according to schedule, until Gus made the typo."

"Gus?! Who is Gus?" She stiffened, and quickly scanned the room. "Are there more ghosts in here?"

"No," Jason laughed, "Gus isn't here now."

"Will he show up later? Am I going to be haunted by him, too?"

"I see Gus most every day, sometimes more than once, but I doubt that he'll ever show himself to you."

"You doubt? Don't you know for sure?"

"There's a lot I don't know about this spirit thing," he admitted. "In fact, all I do know is what Gus has told me, and a little I've figured out for myself."

Samantha relaxed again, having satisfied herself there were no other visitors present. "I'll probably be sorry for asking, but who is this Gus character?"

"Gus is . . . well . . . he's sort of my probation officer."

"Probation officer? Are you a criminal?"

"No, Sam. I give you my word, I'm one of the good guys. The probation officer bit is just an inside joke. Actually, he has an official title. I just never use it."

"He has a title?"

"Yeah. Special Conditions Coordinator, I think it is."

"You think? You're not sure of much, are you?"

"Come on, Sam. I told you I'm not very good at this spirit thing. I'm doing the best I can."

"I'm not very good at this spirit thing either," she replied. "You have to understand how strange all this is to me. I never believed in ghosts, until now." *In fact,* she thought, *I still wonder if you're not just a short circuit somewhere in my mind.*

"Am I moving too fast?"

"Too fast? Yesterday I was living a simple schoolteacher's life, today I'm being courted by a ghost. I'd say that's just a little fast, wouldn't you?"

Looking down to the floor and brushing a hand across his chin, he appeared to be in deep thought. "I'll tell you what," he said in a bit. "I'll cut you a deal."

"A deal? What sort of deal?"

"Would it help," he asked, "if I went away for a while? You know, just to give you some time to sort things out? Of course," he was quick to add, "you have to give me your word. . ."

"To let you come back and finish your story?"

"Will you give your word?"

"When would you come back?"

"That's up to you. How much time do you want?"

"A year?"

"Sam . . . !"

"Okay, how about a week?"

He nodded his head. "That's fair. Do I have your word on it?"

"Do I have a choice?"

"I won't leave until I get your word."

"You'll be back next Saturday?"

"You can count on it."

"Okay, you have my word. But don't show up before noon."

"I know, you and your Saturday mornings." He moved to the door, then stopped.

"Before I go, there is one last thing I just have to tell you."

"I've made it this far, I guess I can handle one last thing."

"I want to tell you how I feel about you."

"How you feel about me? You have feelings?"

"Of course I have feelings. That *never* changes."

"Well?"

"This isn't easy for me."

"Just open your mouth and push out the words, one at a time. How hard can that be?"

He took another deep breath, gazed deep into her eyes, and just said it. "I love you, Sam!"

"You *what?*" she choked. "You can't be serious!"

"Forgive the pun, but yes, I'm dead serious."

She broke out laughing.

"The pun wasn't that funny."

"I'm sorry," she answered covering her mouth to mute the laughter. "I just can't help laughing at how absurd this all sounds."

"I do love you, Sam! I've loved you since you were a little girl."

"Since I was a . . . how long have you been haunting me, anyway?"

"I'm not haunting you!"

"How long?!"

"I've been around since you were five years old, back in 1973."

"You've been watching me since I was five years old?"

"I've been very close to you since then. Closer than you know."

"Why 1973?"

"That's the year I died."

"Oh! . . . I'm. . . "

"Hey, it's okay. It doesn't bother me."

"How did you . . . how did it happen?"

"It was in Vietnam."

"Were you a soldier?"

"I was in the army. I was never good at killing people, so they made me a mess sergeant."

"You were a cook?"

"If that's what you want to call it, yes, I was a cook. A very good cook, I might add."

"Were you killed in the war?"

"Let's just say I died in an accident and let it go at that, okay?"

"I find that very sad," she said in a gentle voice.

"There's nothing to be sad about. Everyone has to die sometime. Under circumstances other than mine, it can be a good experience."

"You call dying a good experience?"

"It can be. Take your grandparents, for instance. I've never seen two happier people than they are, together."

"You've seen them?"

"Many times."

"Oh, boy," Samantha said shaking her head. "This gets stranger by the minute." She looked deeply into Jason's eyes. For the first time she found herself wanting to believe he was real. Thoughts of her grandparents being together and happy filled her heart with overwhelming joy.

Jason took a big breath and let it out slowly. "I guess I'd better be going now," he said with obvious reluctance. "I think it would be better if you turn your back."

"Why should I?"

"I don't want you passing out again when I step through the closed door."

"Do you have to do that? Can't you just sort of vanish or something?"

"No, it doesn't work that way. Once you've seen me with adult eyes, I can never be invisible to you again."

"That's not the way it works in all the ghost movies I've seen."

"Well, that's the way it works with me. At least according to Gus."

"Never let it be said we doubted your probation officer. I'll slip into the bedroom and let you do your wall thing alone."

Stepping to the bedroom door, she paused and asked another question. "By the way, since you've been here all these years, have you ever . . . you know . . . been in my bedroom?"

"Are you asking if I've taken advantage of you because I was unseen?"

"Well, the question does come to mind."

"I have to admit," he answered candidly, "there have been times when the temptation was there. You are a 'looker,' you know. But to answer your question, no. I've always respected your privacy."

"Thank you," she said softly. "It seems you can be a gentleman, even if you are a ghost."

"Sam . . . !"

"If you want to force your presence on me, you might as well accept the fact that I think of you as one of two things. You're either a dirty trick my own mind is playing on me, or you're a ghost."

"See you next week, Sam," he said disgustedly.

She stepped inside her bedroom and closed the door. There on the floor she noticed the revolver she had dropped the night before. Picking it up, she examined it closely. It really was rusty. She had never noticed before. Using both thumbs, she tried to pull the hammer back; it wouldn't budge. *Grandad,* she thought, *you really didn't trust me, did you?*

CHAPTER FIVE

Over the years Samantha had seen many changes in her life—some expected, some not. But she had never experienced anything as traumatic as her encounter with the ghost. Her whole outlook on life was forced to change because of him. She found herself facing a very big question: Was he real, or was he imagined? If he was real, how could he be rationally explained? If he was a trick in her mind, that would be even worse. How could she continue teaching her school children, if she was losing her hold on reality? By Monday afternoon she could stand it no longer. As usual, she turned to the one man in her life for help.

Interrupted by the buzzer, Bruce's attention shifted from the note pad in his hand to the flashing light on his intercom. "Yes, Ms. Bates?" he responded.

"There's someone here to see you, sir," the pleasant female voice replied.

He noted the time. It was exactly four thirty-five. "A walk-in at this time of day, Ms. Bates? You know it's not my policy to take clients after four. Of course, if it's an emergency . . . is it an emergency?"

"I hope not, sir, but I'm sure you'll find time for this client. By the way, the ring on her finger is gorgeous!"

"Samantha is here?" he asked in a burst of excitement.

"Yes sir, and looking quite beautiful I might add."

His hand shot to the center left desk drawer. Pulling out a mirror, he gave himself a quick once-over, adjusted the knot on his tie, and carefully brushed back his hair.

"Send her right in!" he said, cramming the mirror back and closing the drawer with his knee.

Rushing across the room, he met her at the door with a kiss.

"Samantha, darling," he asked, holding her loosely at the shoulders, "why have you come by?"

"Do I need a special reason? What's the matter, afraid I'll find you with another woman?"

"Don't be silly. You know perfectly well you're the only woman in my life."

"Lighten up," she smiled, playfully pushing him away. "I was only making a joke."

"Some things should not be joked about," he said, assuming a fatherly tone. "You should learn to take life more seriously."

"What am I ever going to do with you, Bruce?" she teased. "I can see I have my work cut out for me. You have no idea what life is really all about."

"What are you talking about, Samantha?"

"I have to find a way to improve that stuffy attitude of yours. You need to learn that life is much too important to be taken so seriously."

"That's nonsense. It makes no sense at all."

"Are you going to invite me to sit down, or should I just stand here the rest of the afternoon?"

"Oh, sorry, darling," he apologized, pointing to the sofa.

"Oh no you don't! You're not getting me on that couch. I'm not one of your clients." Crossing the room, she circled his large mahogany desk where she sat in his personal chair. "Wow!" she said. "This is great. How do you get any work done? I'd think you'd fall asleep in this chair."

He cleared his throat and tried to sound very professional. "I'm glad you like the chair, darling. It's part of the image I try to project for the sake of my clients. It bolsters their confidence in me."

While he was speaking, he moved to the front of the desk and looked lovingly across at her. "I was just about ready to close things up here, anyway. What do you say to an early dinner?"

"Sounds great. I'm starved. First, though, I have something I need to talk to you about."

"Certainly, darling. You know I'm always here for you when you need to talk."

She leaned back in the chair and, with a gentle push, swiveled it around to face the picture window behind the desk. "You really live a rough life," she said, admiring the panoramic view of the city. "Fine cars, luxurious houses, an office like this. What would it be like?"

"Everything I have is yours. It only takes one word from you."

"Believe me, it is tempting," she sighed, still looking through the window. "I'm sure in time you'll hear me say that word." Slowly she turned back and noticed the anticipation in his face. She broke out laughing. "Don't get excited, Bruce. That's not what I want to talk to you about today."

He sat down in the chair at the front of the desk, disappointment flashing in his eyes. "Oh, darling, how I wish that had been why you came. But," he sighed, "since it's not, what is it you would like from me?"

"I need a favor."

"A favor? Certainly, darling. Ask anything."

At that moment they were interrupted by the buzzer on his intercom. Reaching across the desk, he pressed the switch. "Yes, Ms. Bates?"

"Mr. Johnson is here to talk to you about the lease on the office. Would you like me to send him in, sir?"

He glanced at Samantha, still in his chair. "Uh, no, Ms. Bates. I'll come out there. All that's needed is my signature on a contract, is it not?"

"That's correct, sir."

"Will you excuse me for a few minutes, darling?"

"Go sign your contract. I'll just sit here and enjoy the view from your window."

Samantha enjoyed watching the activity in the city below. Everything looked so tiny, almost unreal. Before long, thoughts of the ghost began to creep to the forefront of her mind. Thoughts she had wrestled with for the better part of the last two days. He claimed to have been with her since she was a child. As a girl, and later as a woman, she had often felt as if someone unseen was near. Was it possible that he had really been there, and that she somehow had sensed him?

"Are you listening to me, darling?"

"Oh—I'm sorry, Bruce. I was deep in thought. I didn't hear you come back in. Did you say something to me?"

"I was asking about the favor you wanted."

"Oh yes, the favor. I could use your help with a school project. You're always telling me how good your lawyer friend, Philip Morgan, is at detective work."

At the mention of Philip's name, Bruce's face lit up. "Philip Morgan," he repeated. "He's the best detective I've ever seen. When we were in college together, he kept everyone in stitches with his little blackmail pranks. If there was some dirt to be found, no matter how deep it was buried, Philip would find it." Bruce looked at Samantha with a puzzled smile on his face. "What in the world could you possibly need from Philip?" he asked.

"I was wondering . . . would he have access to old military records?"

"Of course he would, darling. What exactly is it you want?"

"My class is doing a study on the Vietnam conflict."

"Isn't that a strange subject for a fifth-grade class?"

"Of course not," she said, defending herself. "These kids are never too young to learn about our nation's history."

"I suppose not," he shrugged.

"Anyway," she continued, "one of my students brought in a story of a relative who supposedly was killed in Vietnam in 1973. I would like to substantiate the story and learn anything else I can about the man. It could be very interesting for the class."

"I think you're right, it does sound interesting. No wonder those children love you so much. Almost as much as I do, I suppose."

"Do you think Philip could help?"

"No question about it." Bruce picked up a note pad and pen from his desk. "Tell me everything you know about the man."

"His name is Jason Hackett. He was a soldier in the army, and he died in 1973."

"That's all you know?"

"That's it, except I know he died in Vietnam. In some kind of an accident, I think. Oh, and one other thing. He was a mess sergeant."

"It's not much to go on, but I'll give you ten-to-one odds that Philip will find him. How soon do you need this?"

"Oh, I don't know. A week or so?"

"I'll call him in the morning."

"Thanks, Bruce." She rose and moved to where he was standing. "I owe you a big one, sport," she said, with a kiss and tight squeeze to his neck.

"That kind of thing will get a favor out of me anytime," he said, returning the kiss.

"By the way," he asked, changing the subject, "how did you get from the school to my office?"

"How do you think I got here? I took a taxi."

"Why do you insist on traveling this dangerous city in taxi cabs and buses?"

"A poor ride beats a good walk any day," she laughed.

"You know perfectly well I'll drop whatever I'm doing and pick you up anytime."

"Even if I am only a schoolteacher," she scoffed, "I can afford a taxi now and then."

"I've offered time and again to buy you a car. Why are you so stubborn?"

"You're doing it again, Bruce—treating me like a child."

"I'm not treating you like a child! Why can't you see? It's just not safe for a woman alone to ride a taxi cab in this city."

"You'll never learn, will you?"

"I'll never learn what, darling?"

"That I need some room to breathe. If you really want to marry me, you'll have to stop smothering me."

"But, Samantha. . . "

"Bruce! If I do marry you, I expect to be treated like a wife, not like a child! Now, are you still in the mood to feed a hungry schoolteacher?"

"More than ever," he sighed.

"Then let's do it!" Sliding her arm through his, she led the way to the door. "I'm in the mood for Chinese food tonight, Bruce."

He forced a grin. "That sounds great, darling."

As the door closed, it sent a rush of air that exposed the top sheet of a memo pad on the desk. On it, Bruce had written, "Convince yourself, the next time you see Samantha, to tell her how much you hate Chinese food."

CHAPTER SIX

The next Saturday morning, as the first rays of sunlight flooded her bedroom window, Samantha found herself wide awake. "I can't believe this," she groaned. "Why can't I sleep when I have the chance?"

Refusing to admit her anxiety over the possible return of the ghost, she lay tossing and turning for half an hour. It was useless. Every thought returned to him. Finally, realizing it was impossible to get back to sleep, she dragged herself out of bed. *Wouldn't you know it?* she thought in disgust. *The one Saturday morning Bruce didn't call, and this happens to me.*

She found herself rushing her shower, which was completely out of character. "I have to get that ghost off my mind," she told herself. "He probably won't show up, anyway. I should admit it, I only imagined him in the first place."

By ten that morning the uneasiness became too much. She decided to leave the apartment for awhile. She needed some groceries anyway. The trip to and from the store was pleasant, and for once the bus was on time both ways. The elevator was even working, sparing her having to lug the groceries up seven flights.

By the time the afternoon sun had reached the one small window in the front part of her apartment, her regular Saturday work schedule was finished. She fell to the sofa with a *Newsweek* she had picked up that morning and tried to do some reading. She couldn't concentrate, though, and soon gave up on the idea.

Tossing the magazine aside, Samantha glanced through the window and thought how lovely the day had turned out. The trees in the quaint little park across the street were shimmering with a fresh crop of tender spring leaves. The surface of the lake glistened like a thousand tiny diamonds as a gentle breeze formed ripples reflecting the soft afternoon light. The peaceful scene beckoned her.

Five minutes later she was enjoying the crisp afternoon air as she strolled leisurely along the walk bordering the lake. Sunlight filtered through the ruffling leaves, producing a myriad of dancing shadows on the surface of the walkway. The beauty of the moment was breathtaking.

She stopped at one of her favorite spots on the lake's edge, opened a bag of bread crumbs, and tossed a few into the water. In a matter of seconds, the first white duck arrived to enjoy the treat. As she threw more crumbs, other ducks hurried to the scene. Soon the lake was alive with noisy birds, each competing for its share of the bread.

If it wasn't for this ghost thing, she thought, *I could be enjoying an afternoon like this very much.* As the day progressed with no sign of the ghost, she became more certain that she had imagined the whole thing. *Maybe it's better that way after all,* she reasoned. *It's easier explained than a ghost. And perhaps if I get a little more rest, it will never happen again.*

"Hi, Sam . . . how was your week?"

She whirled at the sound of his voice. Her heart pounded violently. "Oh, no!" she gasped. "You did come back!"

"Missed me that much, huh?"

"Like I'd miss a toothache," she answered, trying to regain her normal heartbeat.

"Well, I hope you made good use of your painless week, but I told you I'd be back, didn't I?"

"I was hoping you lied."

"Not me, Sam. I wouldn't lie to you."

The clamoring of the ducks became louder as they grew impatient for more bread crumbs. She threw the last of the bread into the water, creating a frenzy of flapping feathers.

"I still don't believe in you. I don't know why, but for some reason my mind is making you up."

"Thanks, that's a real morale booster."

"I talked to Bruce about you, too. He agrees you don't exist."

"Come on, Sam. We both know you wouldn't mention me to that wimp, and even if you did, it wouldn't make any difference. I'm still real."

Turning to the lake, she watched the ducks finish off the last of the treat. Realizing the handout was over, one by one they swam away.

"I wish you were that easy to get rid of," she said, facing him again. "All I had to do was ignore them."

"Yeah, well, I'm no duck. You'd better get used to having me around. Gus tells me I have to stick to you like iron on a magnet, until. . . "

"Until what?"

"Until the mess he made with his typo gets straightened out and I can finally go through the bright door."

"Bright door?" she gasped. "You just keep coming up with these new things!"

"I'm sorry, Sam, I don't mean to confuse you. I just don't know what else to call it. You see," he said, searching for the right words, "whenever someone dies, this bright door just sort of . . . opens up."

"A bright door opens up when someone dies?"

"Yeah, that's right."

"Opens up to where?"

"I'm not sure. All I ever got to see was a long tunnel of light, leading off into the distance."

"Why didn't you go through the door?" Samantha asked, shocked at her own question.

"I started to, but Gus stopped me."

"Let me guess. You have to convince me to bake you a plum pudding, or something like that, before you can go through the bright door. Right?"

"No, Sam," he laughed. "I wish it was that simple, but there's more to it than plum pudding. My destiny has to be set straight before I go through the door."

Suddenly, Samantha's attention was drawn to a group of boys playing football a few yards away. "What are they laughing at?"

Jason glanced back at the boys. "They think you're talking to yourself," he chuckled. "They can neither see nor hear me."

"Why can't they see you?" she demanded.

"It's the rules. You, Sam, are the only one I can show myself to."

"Oh, no! I must look like an idiot to those boys."

"Face the lake. They'll think you're trying to attract the ducks again."

She quickly spun around. "I think I hate you!" she sneered.

"Hate me? Hey, none of this is my fault. If it hadn't been for the typo, things would have been very different."

"What is this typo you keep bringing up?"

"The typo is what started it all. It happened because Gus's secretary took a day off."

"He has a secretary?"

"Of course he has a secretary, but she took that morning off. You have to understand Gus. He has no patience whatsoever. He wanted to finish a hot project, so instead of waiting until she returned the next day, he typed it himself."

"Gus uses a typewriter?"

"Actually it's a computer. An incredibly elaborate computer that does things you can't even imagine. One thing it can't do, though, is correct typing errors, and Gus has about as much typing skill as he has patience."

Samantha glanced over her shoulder at the boys, who had lost interest in her. Just in case, she remained facing the lake. "This is awkward," she said, "talking with you behind me."

"That's easy to fix," he replied. He simply walked out onto the lake, until he was standing in front of her. "There, how's that?"

"What are you doing?" she shrieked.

"I'm just making it easier for us to talk. Isn't that what you wanted?"

"No! I can't handle these little tricks of yours. Get back over there where you look more natural."

"Sorry, Sam," he said, scurrying back to the grass. "I didn't know that would bother you."

Samantha's shouting caught the boys' attention again. Blushing, she turned and walked briskly away. Jason followed.

Once out of sight of the boys, she tossed the empty bread sack into a trash container and scowled at the ghost.

"I said I was sorry, didn't I?"

"All right," she said, stepping under the shade of a fruitless mulberry tree. "Let's try it again. I want to hear about the typo, but keep your feet planted on the ground, okay?"

"Okay," he agreed, and then resumed the story. "You see, Sam, when Gus made the typo, he was working on a special contract that affects the two of us."

"What do you mean, the two of us?"

"You and me. The contract he was working on is one that links our destinies together."

"Hold it right there!" she snapped. "What right does Gus have tinkering with my destiny?"

"That's his job."

"He interferes with people's destinies?"

"No! He manages special contracts that affect the destinies of certain people."

"You expect me to believe your friend Gus has a piece of paper linking my destiny to a ghost?"

"I'm not a ghost!"

"Don't raise your voice at me!"

"All right, I'm sorry I raised my voice, but I hate it when you call me that. As for the contract, yes, Gus has it."

"Okay then, I have a question for you. If our destinies are linked, why did you live at a different time than me?"

"That's what I'm trying to tell you, Sam. If it wasn't for the typo, we would have lived our lifetimes together. Gus typed 1926, where he should have typed 1962. Don't you see . . . I should have been born in 1962. Instead, I was born thirty-six years too soon, and here we are."

Samantha was dumfounded. "You're serious about this, aren't you?" she asked.

"I've never been more serious in my, pardon the expression, life. Gus assures me he can fix it, if he has a little more time."

"Does fixing it involve interfering with my future?"

"Yes, and no. If the contract is to be honored, it has to include you. On the other hand," he said, kicking at the ground with one foot, "the contract can be terminated. In that case, you're completely free of me."

Samantha thought a moment about the things she had just

heard. "Look, uh. . ." She paused and rolled her hand, as if not knowing what to call him.

"My name is Jason."

She couldn't bring herself to call him by a name. Calling him by name would imply she accepted his presence, something she was not yet willing to do.

"Look," she said, "I want to be perfectly honest with you. I'm not at all sure you exist, and if you do, I'm not sure I believe your story. Just for the sake of argument, however, let's say it is true. What would be wrong with the second choice, terminating the contract? That would allow you and me both to get on with our lives."

"Nothing, I suppose," he choked. "Except it would break my heart. I told you before, I'm in love with you."

There was a park bench a few feet away from where they were standing. He walked there and sat down. Samantha paused a moment, then she followed, and sat next to him.

"Sam, do you know what you just did?"

"What did I do?"

"You broke your ground rule."

"I guess I did, didn't I? Would you like me to move?"

"No! But aren't you afraid of me anymore?"

"No, I can see you're harmless. A big inconvenience, but harmless, nevertheless. Besides, I needed to sit down after everything you've hit me with. First you tell me you're courting me. Next you add the little fact that you love me. Now you spring this destiny and typo thing on me."

"You can add a few new facts to your list, Sam. I love the way your hair bounces when you walk, and the way your face lights up when you smile. I love the dimple that shows in your chin when you're angry. I love how your eyes sparkle when you laugh. Sam, you are the most beautiful woman I have ever seen."

"Thank you," she answered. "That's the best compliment I've ever had, from a ghost." His mouth flew open to speak, but she cut him off. "I know, you don't like me calling you a ghost. Consider yourself out of luck on that one, and tell me what else it is you want from me."

"What do I want?" he sighed. "I want you to get to know me a little better. I think you'll learn to like me, if you give me a chance."

"Do I have a choice?"

"Not really, I suppose. Does that bother you?"

She didn't answer, but studied him intently for a long time. Finally she spoke. "Would you mind," she asked, "if I tried to touch you?"

He was taken aback. "No, of course I wouldn't mind, but. . . "

"Let me try, okay?"

"Suit yourself, Sam."

Slowly, she extended her hand toward his face, and laid it alongside where his cheekbone should have been. He was right. She felt nothing.

"Are you satisfied now?"

"I'm satisfied that you're either a trick in my mind, or you really are a ghost."

"You're impossible," he said, standing up and glaring down at her.

"*I'm* impossible? Maybe you'd better take stock of who's haunting who here!"

She rose and started walking slowly back toward her apartment building. Jason remained close. "I'm not sure," she said, "whether to be angry with you or complimented by your attention. I have to admit, I feel a little flattered. On the other hand, I'm really ticked that your sidekick thinks he can fool around with my destiny."

"Look," Jason said, moving in front of her and coming to a stop. "I'm not insensitive to what you're going through because of me. I really wish there was something I could do to make it easier. I know you doubt that I'm real, and I'd give anything if I had a way of proving myself, but I don't know what it would be."

"Maybe I'll find a way to prove you're imagined. You would be easier to deal with that way. I'm toying with the idea of telling the whole story to Bruce. After all, it is his profession to deal with things like this."

"Dumb idea," Jason said, stepping out of her way again. "If you think he treats you like a child now, try telling him about me."

Samantha shot a puzzled look at Jason as she resumed walking. "How do you know he treats me like a child?"

"I told you, I've been around a very long time."

"On my dates?"

"Some of them."

"How dare you!"

"Try to see it from my perspective. I had to look out for my best interest, Sam. Besides, I only went along on a few, and then only with Bruce."

"If you don't beat all. I'm glad I can at least see you now."

"So am I," he quickly agreed.

"I suppose," she said, after thinking things out, "I have no choice but to find a way of dealing with you."

"That's right. I can't go anywhere until Gus figures out what to do. Not only for my sake, but for his as well. His mistake has gotten him in real trouble with the higher authorities."

"Higher authorities? I thought that Gus was the top man."

"Oh, no! He's just a little twig on the tree. The higher authorities could set the typo straight in an instant, if they wanted to. They refused, though. They told Gus that since he got himself into the mess, he could figure a way to get himself out of it."

"Well, I've got to admit, this crazy story has caught my interest. Tell me how Gus thinks he can straighten things out."

"I wish you could know Gus. He's the grandaddy of all hustlers. He's always trying to work a deal. He'll find a way. I guarantee it. He has one deal going right now, but I hesitate to mention it. It's really far out."

"Try me," she chuckled. "It couldn't be much worse than what I've heard already."

"Want to bet?"

"Come on, tell me."

"Okay, but remember, you asked for it. He's trying to find me another body."

"He's what?!"

"I warned you, Sam."

"You are kidding, of course—aren't you?"

"I'm serious. Gus says if he could work it right . . . finding some guy just ready to cash in his chips, he might be able to pull it off."

"Might?"

"Well, it's never been done before. Gus is not sure exactly how it would work."

"How reassuring."

"I suggested he find a way to let me have Bruce's body."

"That's sick. You really didn't say that, did you?"

"Yes, I did! With his body and my great personality, you couldn't help being attracted to me."

"You're insane! You've absolutely lost it!"

"You sound just like Gus. That's about what he said."

Reaching the crosswalk, Samantha pressed the "walk" button and waited for a green light.

"There is another answer to this whole thing," Jason continued, "but I really hate it."

"I'm not sure I want to hear this one."

Jason ignored her remark. "I can keep the contract valid by waiting, on this side of the bright door, until you live out your normal life. We could get together at that time, with no trouble at all."

"And you'll be haunting me the rest of my life? That sounds like a great option!" she sneered.

"Look at it from my side. How do you think I'd feel hanging around for another fifty or so years, watching you with that pompous shrink?"

"I really don't know. I have to deal with what's real. Whether or not I marry Bruce is my decision, and mine only. Not you, or this so-called Gus, can change that."

"You're right, Sam. I can't stop you from marrying Bruce. If you did, it would kill me, but I can't stop you."

"Kill you?"

"Figuratively speaking, of course."

"You're not invited on the honeymoon, either. I deserve some privacy, even from a ghost. Come to think of it," she added, "that should be *especially* from a ghost."

"I get the picture, Sam. If it ever comes to that, you'll get your privacy. I give you my word on it."

The green walk light came on, and together they crossed the street. "Sorry I can't get the door for you, Sam," Jason shrugged as they reached the entrance to the building.

"At least the thought was there," she said, pushing it open herself.

"I don't suppose you'd consider letting me come up and watch television with you awhile?" Jason asked hopefully.

She stopped in front of the elevator and stared at him. "You're getting a little pushy, aren't you? Just because I listened to your story doesn't mean I'm giving you a green light to get friendly with me."

"You can't blame me for trying, can you?"

"I guess you have that right, and I might consider it sometime. Tonight, however, I have a date with Bruce. He's picking me up at five."

She pressed the elevator call button. While waiting, she took a close look at Jason, whose change of expression left little doubt how he was feeling. "Look," she said. "I am engaged to Bruce, and I have every right to date him without your interference. If you intend to haunt me, stay out of my personal life."

"I'll do my best, Sam. I've told you my story, and all I want is a chance to make a case for myself. There's no other way to do that but to stay close to you."

"I suppose I can live with that, if I have to. So long as you show me some respect, that is."

"There are a few more things I'd like to explain. May I come up to your apartment? Just until Bruce arrives, that is."

"Do I have your word you'll leave as soon as I ask, without giving me any trouble?"

"Word of honor, Sam."

"All right," she said, "I'm going to trust you, this once. Don't make me sorry I did."

CHAPTER SEVEN

While Samantha waited for the elevator to come down, she studied the figure standing next to her. *How can this be happening?* she asked herself. *Seven days ago, no one could have convinced me to believe in a ghost. Now, I'm either standing next to one, or I'm losing my mind.* The hint of a smile crossed her lips as she realized she wanted him to be real. In fact, strange as it seemed, she actually liked the fellow, though he certainly did create some problems for her. One thing was for sure: life would never be as simple as it was before he came along.

To Samantha's relief, the elevator responded and the doors slid open. "Amazing," she said, stepping inside. "That's twice today this thing's been good to me. Maybe it's afraid of ghosts," she laughed. "If that's the case, you can stay around for that reason alone."

Jason followed her into the car. "That's one advantage I have," he smiled. "I don't need vehicles of any kind to get where I want to go."

She pressed another button, and the car began its noisy ascent. The sound of a monotonous "ker-plunk—ker-plunk—ker-plunk" repeated over and over. She had to shout to be heard over the noise. "I'm curious. How do you travel from one place to another?"

"It's hard to explain," he shouted back. "I hardly know how it works myself. I just sort of think about where I want to go, and 'zap,' there I am."

"You can go up seven flights of stairs, just like that?"

"Child's play."

"What I would give to have the ability to do that! Especially when this elevator decides to take a rest."

"That's no problem," Jason teased. "You can have that, if you want it. You can get it the same way I did."

"Forget it!" she shuddered. "I'll climb the stairs."

Her ears were still ringing as she unlocked the door to her

apartment. Glancing back, she expected to see Jason behind her. He wasn't there. She searched the hall in both directions, but he was nowhere to be seen.

"All right!" she said. "What are you up to now?" No answer. Slowly she opened the door, stepped inside, and glanced around. There he stood, a sly grin across his face.

"Stop that!" she snapped. "You startled me!"

"Sorry, I wasn't thinking." The mischievous twinkle in his eye betrayed how much he had enjoyed his little prank.

"Well, the least you could do is knock before you come in. That's only common courtesy."

His voice softened. "You're probably right. But angels don't knock."

She leveled a curious gaze at him. "Oh, so that's what you call yourself—not a ghost, but an angel?"

"Well, I guess you could say. . ."

"You mean something like my, uh, *guardian* angel?"

He grinned again. "Aha! Now you're beginning to catch on."

"Well, I hope you understand, mister ghost-angel, that you do take a bit of getting used to. And just for the record, I still see you as more of a ghost than an angel."

"Whatever." He followed her into the kitchen, where she invited him to sit at the small table.

"Would you mind moving the chair out for me?" he asked.

She looked startled. "You mean to tell me you can't move your own chair?"

"Believe it or not, that's the way it is."

"I always thought ghosts could make things fly through the air, and do other scary things of that sort."

"Hollywood ghosts do those things, Sam. I'm not a Hollywood ghost."

She moved the chair, and with a grin of her own asked a question. "What kind of ghost are you, then?"

"You never give up, do you?"

"I guess that makes us even then, doesn't it?"

"Even for what?"

"For your sick prank at the door."

Jason glared at her a moment, then began to laugh. She joined in and they laughed together.

"Can I get you . . . uh . . . anything?" Without thinking she had let the words slip out. She felt very foolish.

"Thanks for the thought, but I don't eat the same things you do. Not anymore."

"You eat?"

"Of course I eat."

"But . . . ?"

"Gus brings me sack lunches," he chuckled.

"You really shouldn't laugh at me. After all, I've never known a ghost before."

"Looks like I'm going to have to get used to you calling me that, doesn't it?"

"Looks that way," she grinned. "The walk in the park left me thirsty. Do you mind if I have a soda?"

"Of course I don't mind, Sam. I'll even have one with you. One of my own, that is."

Her eyes narrowed, but she made no response. Turning to the cupboard she reached for a glass, then filled it with ice from the freezer. Glancing in his direction, she was astonished to see he did have a drink on the table in front of him.

"Well, I'll be. You weren't kidding, were you?"

"Would a respectable departed person like myself kid about a thing like that?"

"Where did it come from? How did you do that?"

"Gus brought it to me."

"Gus?"

"Yeah, he can be an okay guy at times."

"Is he here now?"

"No, he's gone. He's fast when he wants to be."

"You enjoy springing these little surprises on me, don't you?"

"No, of course not."

"Liar!"

"Okay, I give up. I suppose I do enjoy it, just a little."

Looking at this strange person sitting at her table, Samantha took further stock of her own feelings. She had to admit, she wanted to know more about him, and she wanted to know more about his friend, Gus. "If Gus comes and goes so quickly," she asked, "where is it he bounces off to?"

"I've told you before, the other side of the bright door."

"You've told me nothing about the other side of your so-called bright door," she said, moving things around in the refrigerator, searching for a soda.

"Don't know anything."

"Gus must have told you something."

"A little, I guess, but not much."

She found a can of Orange Crush at the back of the top shelf. Stretching to her limit, she just managed to reach it. "Tell me what you know about it," she said.

"You're starting to get curious about me, aren't you?"

"A little, I suppose," she blushed. "But then, isn't that what you wanted me to do?"

"It is," he grinned.

"Then answer my question," she said, closing the refrigerator door while juggling the soda in one hand and the glass of ice in the other.

Jason slipped into deep thought a moment before he answered. "According to Gus, it's not too much different from here. Except, he keeps telling me, everything is on a higher level over there."

"Higher level?"

"I think he means the elevators never break down, and that sort of thing."

"Sounds good to me," she answered, pulling the tab on her soda can.

"I know from my own experience that things don't change at death. I kept my personality, my thoughts, my ideas, everything that makes me who I am. Gus says it's the same with everyone. The difference over there is they're on a higher level. They can love stronger, feel greater happiness, and live life more fully. Does that make any sense?"

"It does," she answered. "I never thought much about it before, but yes, it makes perfect sense. Tell me more."

"I wish I could, Sam. Unfortunately, that's about all I know."

The sparkling orange liquid ran smoothly over the cubes of ice as she filled her glass. "So," she asked, "you were born in 1926?"

"August fifteenth, to be exact."

"You should have been born in 1962, is that right?"

"Yes, that's it exactly."

"And you died in 1973?"

"In Vietnam."

Samantha quickly figured he would have been forty-seven years old at the time of his death—a little old, she felt, for the typical soldier in the Vietnam conflict. "Were you a career soldier?" she asked.

"Sort of, I suppose. I liked to cook, and they gave me my chance in the army, so I just hung around."

"You died in an accident?"

"Yes."

"Mortar shell explosion?"

"No."

"Sniper fire?"

"No, Sam."

"Well, what then?"

"It's not important."

"Come on, tell me," she pressed. "How did you die?"

"Like I said, Sam, it's not important."

Her curiosity burned for an answer, but it was obvious he was not going to give one. Reluctantly, she changed the subject. "If you've been haunting me, or whatever you want to call it, since 1973, why did you wait so long to show yourself?"

"Believe me, I didn't want to; it was Gus's idea. He said the time was never right, until now. I waited over twenty years. I don't know how you feel about seeing me, but from my point of view, it's about time."

Samantha sipped her drink and set the glass gently back on the table. "Assuming you are real, what exactly do you plan on doing next?"

"I plan to make the most out of whatever time I have."

"Make the most in what respect?"

"In courting you. I'm going to give Bruce the fight of his life."

"Isn't that a little foolish? There's no way I could marry you, even if I wanted to."

"Gus is working on that part. My biggest goal, right now, is to get you to like me. I'll worry about the rest when the time comes."

"You should know, right up front, that I intend to make Bruce part of my future. Wouldn't you be better off just to let go, right now?"

"Can't do that, Sam."

"Why not?"

"I'm in love with you, and I've seen the contract that says we belong together. I have one shot to keep that contract valid, and I have to take that shot. If I end up hurt, then so be it. I could never forgive myself if I didn't at least try."

"There's no way I can talk you out of this?"

"No, Sam. There's no way."

"All right, but remember I told you up front how things are. No matter how bad things may turn out for you, don't ever try to lay a guilt trip on me."

"No guilt trips, I promise."

"Uh-oh," she gasped, glancing at the clock on the microwave. "Time's getting away. Bruce will be here in less than an hour. You'd better leave now."

"Where's the old boy taking you tonight, shopping for a new couch to go in his office? No, come to think of it, none of his dates are that exciting."

"It's really none of your business, but if you must know, we're going to his friend's house for dinner."

"I never have been able to figure out what you see in that guy."

"That's because you're jealous of him."

"I am not! Well, maybe a little. All right, yes! I am jealous of that wimp. Are you satisfied?"

"You promised not to give me any trouble about leaving."

"I'm going," he said, crossing to the door, where he paused a moment. "Thanks, Sam," he said quietly.

"Thanks for what?" she asked.

"For believing in me."

"I didn't say I believed in you. However, I will give you some thought."

"Well then, thanks for that. It's a lot better than I had last week."

"Please leave now, I'm out of time."

"Can you handle watching me walk through a closed door, or do you want to open it?"

"I won't like it, but I can handle it."

"Well then, for now, goodbye Sam."

"Goodbye . . . to you, too."

"The name's Jason," he said as he turned and stepped through the closed door.

"Goodbye—Jason," she whispered just loud enough that she alone could hear.

CHAPTER EIGHT

"I think you'll find the Morgans fascinating, my dear," Bruce said as he pressed the shiny brass button, sounding the door chimes.

Samantha glanced at her watch and drew a quick breath.

Bruce tensed. "I had hoped you'd be a little more enthusiastic about spending an evening with my friends."

"What makes you think I'm not enthusiastic?"

"It's very obvious."

"Okay, I admit it. This is not my idea of an especially exciting evening."

"You'll have to get used to it, my dear," he said, his voice a pitch deeper than usual. "It goes with the territory when you become Mrs. Vincent."

"So you've told me, Bruce."

Brushing her hair back with his hand, and assuming his "daddy knows best" posture, he continued his lecture. "You must understand, people like the Morgans are important to me. I wouldn't be where I am today without the right social connections."

Samantha studied Bruce closely. Despite his faults, she still thought of him as strikingly handsome. If only his personality could better match his looks. True, some progress over the last six months was evident, but not much. Samantha loved a good challenge, but she had to wonder if this was more than she wanted to face. Could she ever mold Bruce into a man she would be happy to live with the rest of her life? Times like this did nothing to strengthen her hope. Still, she resolved not to give up on him.

The front door opened and Philip Morgan stood smiling at the threshold. "Bruce, my man, how good to see you. And this gorgeous creature," he said, kissing her hand, "must be Samantha."

"I'm Samantha," she answered in a polite, but guarded voice.

"Bruce, you old dog, for once you didn't stretch the truth one bit. She is stunning."

She studied the man's narrow green eyes, which didn't seem to match the rest of his oval face. If Bruce hadn't told her he was a successful lawyer, she would have taken him for a used car salesman. "Thank you, Mr. Morgan," she said, struggling to sound sincere.

"Please, my dear, I'm simply Philip." She bit her lip and nodded a casual yes. Somehow she was able to keep from laughing at his amusing mannerism.

Once inside, Samantha was almost afraid to step on the ivory white carpet for fear her shoes were not clean enough. Philip led the way down three semi-circular steps into a living room that looked like a page out of an interior decorating magazine.

"Please, sit here," he said, pointing to a large green sofa in the center of the room. "Rebecca will join us shortly. She's just putting the finishing touches to dinner. I hope you like roast duck."

"One of my favorites," Bruce nodded briskly.

The sofa proved less comfortable for Samantha than its beauty had suggested. It was custom built for someone much taller. She noticed it fit Bruce just fine.

"Can I get either of you something to drink?"

"Nothing for me," Samantha quickly responded.

Bruce cleared his throat and fumbled with his key ring. "Samantha doesn't drink," he explained in an apologetic tone. "I'd better pass this time, too." Philip looked as if he was about to say something, but thought better of it. He closed the half-opened door to the bar.

Samantha tried to appear poised while she squirmed to find a comfortable position on the sofa. Then she noticed it—a large oil painting, hanging on the far wall across from her. How strangely out of place it seemed with the rest of the room's decor. It depicted what appeared to be a scene of General Custer leading his battered army into their final battle. At that moment, a voice interrupted her thoughts.

"Kind of gets to you, doesn't it, Sam?"

She spun toward the sound of the voice, and gasped.

"What is it, darling? You look as though you've seen a ghost."

Though she didn't answer, that's exactly what she had seen.

"I especially like the horses," Jason continued. "The guy who painted that picture really knew how to do horses."

"Is anything wrong, my dear?" Philip asked, having also noticed Samantha's sudden change of expression.

"What? Oh no—of course not. I was just taken aback by the beauty of the painting."

"Oh yes, my painting. It is a beauty, isn't it? It was one of my first works when I was still in school."

Samantha leaned forward, still struggling to get comfortable on the sofa. "It truly is lovely, Philip," she said through clenched teeth.

"Yes," he agreed, "it's still one of my favorites. I'm afraid, however, Rebecca fails to see the beauty in it. She's opposed its hanging there from the beginning."

Jason broke into laughter, but quickly choked it off when he noticed the look on Samantha's face. "Come on, Sam," he pleaded. "No one else knows I'm here anyway." She glared at him in icy silence.

"Good evening, my dear." Rebecca's lavender gown swished with each step as she crossed the room to where Samantha was sitting. "We've heard so much about you."

Samantha smiled, at least on the outside, and wished she had chosen something to wear other than a shirt and Dockers. Rising as gracefully as possible, she extended a hand, which Rebecca took in both of her own.

"This woman must buy her perfume in quart jars," Jason noted, drawing an evil glance from Samantha.

"Oh, Philip!" Rebecca exclaimed. "Just look at this ring! It's gorgeous, and it's certainly larger than the one you gave me."

"Ha! With all the money I save Bruce on legal fees, he should be able to afford a rock like that."

Turning to Bruce, still seated on the green sofa, the hostess extended the back of her hand. "How's my favorite psychologist?" she asked, sounding like a line from a Marilyn Monroe movie.

He stood and kissed her hand. "I'm doing fine, fair lady. And I must say you look simply beautiful."

"I'm famished!"

"Good," she said. "Let's eat, then."

Bruce slipped his arm through Samantha's as they followed the host and hostess to the dining area. "Is something wrong, darling?" he whispered. "You were acting strange."

"You were right," she whispered back.

"Right about what?"

"I did see a ghost."

He squeezed her arm. "My Samantha and her jokes," he said. "No wonder I love you so much."

"Gag me," came a voice from behind. A voice that none but Samantha heard.

"How delightful!" Samantha exclaimed at first sight of the dining table. "A candlelight dinner."

"I just thought it would add that little something extra," Rebecca boasted while lighting the candles.

Jason entered the room and looked things over for himself. "I don't know," he said. "It looks fancy enough, but the proof is in how it tastes. Offhand, I'd say she burnt the duck." He shrugged at Samantha's obvious look of anger. "Well, it looks burnt to me; and after all, cooking is my expertise."

Visiting the Morgans was not Samantha's idea of a great evening in the first place, and with Jason's little tricks added in, it was growing steadily worse. At least the dining room chair proved more comfortable than that green sofa had been.

"So, my friend," Philip asked while passing the broccoli primavera, "how's things with the old 'couch jockey?'"

Bruce frowned. "You should show more respect for my profession. I detest the use of that wretched phrase."

"I'll remind you of that next time you tell me a lawyer joke."

"That's not the same thing!"

"You must be doing well, Bruce. Other than that soldier you asked me to check up on, you haven't hit me up for any free services lately."

"Free services? Ben Matlock charges less than you, and he's never lost a case."

"Oh, my. How embarrassing." Rebecca had just tasted the duck. "I fear I've managed to burn this."

Jason shrugged his shoulders. "What can I say?"

"Oh, no!" Samantha lied. "The duck is simply delicious."

"Come on, Sam," Jason chided. "Tell her the truth. The duck could pass for Ben Franklin's kite."

"What would an army cook know about . . . ?" Every eye in the room fell on Samantha, and she went stone silent. Nothing this embarrassing had happened to her since high school, when Brad Arnold stole her diary and read several pages over the school loud speaker system before being stopped.

After what seemed a very long time, Bruce broke the silence. "What on earth did you mean by that, darling?"

"Oh—I'm sorry, Bruce. I was just thinking out loud about that army cook. You know, the one you asked Philip to check out for me."

"That Jason fellow, you mean?"

"You asked Bruce to check up on me? What a sneaky thing to do, Sam."

"Yes," Samantha answered, looking at Bruce and not the ghost. "Did you learn anything about him yet?"

"Am I missing something here?" Philip asked. "How did we get on the subject of an army cook?"

Bruce covered his left eye to hide the twitching. "The soldier I asked you to check out, Philip. He was a cook, remember?"

"Oh," Rebecca broke in, "it was Samantha who wanted to know about the soldier? Philip asked me to check it out because I had better access to military files than he did. What would you possibly be interested in a soldier for, my dear?"

Feeling a little better, as the deception seemed to be working, Samantha answered, "I needed information on the man for a project I am doing in my school class."

"You're attending school, then?" Rebecca asked with a puzzled look.

"No, didn't Bruce tell you? I'm a schoolteacher. I teach fifth grade."

"A schoolteacher? That's—a nice profession, I suppose. Does it pay well?"

Samantha's grip tightened angrily around her napkin. "No, Rebecca!" she answered bluntly. "As a matter of fact, it doesn't pay well at all. But it's my chosen career, and I love it."

"I see," Rebecca said with a nauseating grin. "You do know I'm an attorney, do you not?"

"I am aware of that, yes."

"Shame on you, Bruce," Rebecca scolded. "You didn't tell us she was a schoolteacher."

"She makes me ill," Jason sneered. "I didn't like that woman from the first time I saw her."

"Neither did I!" Samantha mumbled under her breath.

"Can't we just let this soldier thing go for now?" Bruce asked, wanting to get as far as possible from the schoolteacher subject.

"No!" Samantha cried. "This is important to me. Did you learn anything about him, Rebecca?"

"Of course I did. I learned a great deal about your Sergeant Jason Hackett."

"He was real?" Samantha gasped. "He actually lived?"

"Why yes, of course he did. He was an army mess sergeant who died in an accident in 1973. January seventh, to be exact."

"Wow, Sam! I'm in the history books! Now do you believe in me?"

"How did he die?" Samantha asked, while glaring at Jason.

"Hey, Sam, let it go. You learned I'm real, that should be good enough."

Rebecca pretended not to hear the question. "Would you like more rice pilaf, Bruce?" she asked.

"Please, Rebecca," Samantha pleaded. "I'd really like to know how the man died."

"Darling," Bruce said, laying a hand gently on her arm, "that's not an appropriate subject for the dinner table."

"Yeah, darling," Jason agreed, "not at the dinner table."

"Stay out of this, Bruce! It's important to me to know how the man died."

"Very well, if you insist," Rebecca continued. "He choked to death on a chicken bone."

"What?" Samantha's face lit up in a devious grin. "He choked on a chicken bone? Was it by any chance from some of his own cooking?"

"You find that funny, Sam? Would you like me better if I'd died like a John Wayne hero?"

"Yes, as a matter of fact it was. He was sampling the food he had prepared for the evening mess. But I must admit, I fail to see why you find this humorous."

"I'm sorry, Rebecca. It seems I was about to make a big mistake in my school class. I planned on using this fellow, Jason, as an example of a war hero. I think I picked a poor example, don't you?"

"I suppose so," Rebecca answered, "but I fail to see what difference it makes."

"So do I," Jason grumbled, walking to the corner of the room to sulk.

"Please," Philip interrupted, "could we talk about something a little more cheerful?"

"Good idea," Bruce agreed. "Tell us about this fascinating new game you want us to play tonight, Rebecca."

"Yes," she beamed, "it does seem to be an interesting game. One of my clients is trying to market it."

Samantha, who loved games of any kind, took interest in the conversation for the first time that evening. "What kind of game?" she asked.

"It's called 'Career Pursuit,'" Rebecca explained. "It's a game of trivia. It sounds like fun, but I need to be more familiar with it. I can't very well help market something I know nothing about, can I?"

Everyone left plenty of room for a generous helping of cherries jubilee. They had pretty well finished off the broccoli primavera, rice pilaf, and sourdough bread, but had hardly touched the roast duck.

Later, in the family room, Rebecca explained the game she had previously set up on a card table. Like many games, it used a board and trivia questions. Several different career choices were available in the game. The higher the career level, the more difficult the questions asked. Of course, higher career levels were allowed to advance further than lesser ones, if the questions were answered correctly.

Having explained the rules, Rebecca passed out a colored token to each player. "Now," she said, "it's time for each of us to pick our career category. I'll take the Professional category, of course. I recommend Bruce and Philip do the same."

"And what," Samantha asked coolly, "do you recommend for me?"

"I suggest, since you're a schoolteacher, you pick an easier category. That will keep the competition closer and make the game a little more fair for you, my dear."

Samantha felt the hair on the back of her neck bristle. "I'll take the same category as the rest of you," she said emphatically.

"As you wish," Rebecca agreed, removing a question card from the stack. "We'll begin with you, Bruce. A man of your background should have little trouble answering this one," she said, glancing at the first question on the card.

She read the question aloud. "'The Berlin Wall came down in the year 1990. What year was it first used to seal off the Soviet Sector?'"

"I thought you said it was going to be an easy question," Bruce complained. "I must admit I don't know the answer for certain, but I will venture a guess. I'll say . . . 1945."

"No!" Samantha burst in. "The wall was first sealed off in August of 1961."

Rebecca's face grew solemn as she checked the answer at the bottom of the card. "I'm stunned," she said. "You answered the year exactly right. The card doesn't give the month."

"It was the middle of August," Samantha beamed. "May I move my token?"

"I'm afraid not, my dear. That question was for Bruce; you move your token only when you answer your own question."

"Oh."

"The second question is on the same subject, and is for Philip. 'What was the complete length of the Berlin Wall?'" After a few minutes of pondering, he had to admit he didn't know.

Samantha made no attempt to hide her delight. "Chalk another one up for the schoolteacher," she squealed. "It was twenty-six and a half miles long."

"Well," Rebecca huffed. "It's obvious we started on a subject you're well acquainted with, Samantha."

"Did you ever stop to think about it? A schoolteacher has to be acquainted with numerous subjects. It goes with the territory," she said, grinning with satisfaction.

"Of course, my dear," Rebecca answered, looking through the stack of cards for just the right one. "Let's see what your question is.

Ah, here's one that will do nicely."

"Weren't there more questions on the first card?" Samantha asked.

"Yes, there were more, but I think we should find a new subject—just to keep the game interesting, of course."

"Oh, of course. We wouldn't want to run a subject into the ground that I made seem so easy, would we?"

"If your concept of a schoolteacher's knowledge is correct, you should have no trouble with this question, my dear."

The question read, "The name *Panthera Pardus* is the scientific name for an animal on the endangered species list. What is the common name for this animal?"

Samantha's mouth went dry, and she felt a knot in the pit of her stomach. At the moment, nothing seemed to matter but proving to this arrogant woman that she was not an ignorant social outcast.

The first two questions had been easy because she had recently studied the subject for her class. But this scientific question was beyond her field of knowledge. She couldn't even venture a respectable guess. Just as she was about to concede in humiliation, he spoke.

"It's a leopard."

She glanced up. There, standing directly behind Rebecca, where he could clearly read the answer on the card, stood Jason.

"A leopard," he said again, "like in a big spotted cat."

Instantly, her face exploded into a smile. *Way to go, you crazy ghost!* she thought.

Then, in a cool, authoritative voice, she gave her answer. "It's a leopard, of course." With silent pleasure, she watched the color drain from Rebecca's face.

You know what, Sam old girl, she thought, *maybe having a ghost around is not such a bad thing after all.* Jason winked at her, and the game went on.

A little after eleven-thirty, three frustrated professionals had to concede the game. Samantha was the undisputed winner.

Her cheery mood told it all. So what if she had had a little outside help in winning the game? That win was more satisfying than eating a big piece of German chocolate cake after a month of dieting.

She even slipped a high sign to the ghost while the others weren't looking. At that moment, Jason was not just any ghost. He was the happiest ghost from here to eternity.

"You seemed to enjoy yourself at the Morgans' after all, darling," Bruce said on the way back to her apartment. His moment of "I told you so" pride was cut short, however, by her reply.

"I want to know, Bruce Vincent, why you are ashamed of my profession."

"What?"

"You deliberately went out of your way to keep from telling them I'm a schoolteacher. Do you mind telling me why?"

"The subject never came up, I suppose."

"It's evident what Rebecca thinks about my profession."

"Samantha, my love, you're reading things into the situation that aren't really there. Rebecca is a lovely woman, and an accomplished attorney."

"My point exactly. She's an accomplished attorney who thinks of me as a lowly schoolteacher."

"You have to admit, darling, Rebecca never had to live in a place like the Anderson Apartments before she married Philip."

"You always have to put a dollar sign on everything, don't you, Bruce?" Samantha folded her arms tightly and stared at the road ahead. "I'm sorry, but I didn't find those people as fascinating as you promised I would. In fact, I think they're a couple of stuffed shirts. Especially Rebecca!"

"Samantha, darling, these people are my friends. You simply must learn to appreciate them, as I do."

Unnoticed in the back seat, a certain ghost remained very quiet and wore a smile so big it had to hurt.

CHAPTER NINE

Samantha soon learned how difficult dealing with a ghost could be. Jason's attitude, however, was a great help. He was not the typical spooky character she might have expected. In fact, he was usually thoughtful, polite, and courteous. Then too, knowing for sure that he was real instead of imagined made things much easier.

Most of the time Jason was willing to live with Samantha's rules, and there were many. For instance, he was never to pop up in her apartment unannounced, and at no time was he allowed in her bedroom. He was to leave promptly if she asked him to go, and he was not supposed to show up at her aerobics class on Tuesday nights. The one rule she had trouble getting him to honor, though, was not to interfere between her and Bruce.

At times it was fun having him around. She especially enjoyed their conversations. Of course, there were other times when she wished things could be like they were before he showed up.

The biggest problem she faced was the uncertainty. Not knowing how this would all end proved frustrating, to say the least. She soon realized that Jason had meant it when he vowed to stay close until Gus could find a suitable solution.

If she asked how Gus was doing on the problem, the answer was always the same. "He's still working on it."

Then there was Bruce. If she were to marry the man, which she was sure she would do in time, he had a right to know about the ghost. On several occasions she had almost given in to the temptation to tell him. Each time, however, fearful of his reaction, she had backed out.

One Friday evening, while Samantha lay on her sofa reading a magazine, Jason's familiar voice called from outside in the hall. "Sam, it's me. May I come in?"

"No, go away. I'm busy right now."

"That's funny, you don't look very busy."

She glanced at the door. There was Jason with only his face inside, and the rest of him still in the hall. "Stop that!" she snapped. "You know how I hate it when you do things like that!"

"May I come the rest of the way in?"

"Okay, but only for a minute or so. I have a date tonight."

"Is the wimp picking you up again?" he asked, fully in the room by this time.

"The wimp, as you're so fond of calling him, happens to be the man I plan to marry."

"I don't like the guy. He bugs me. I hate the way he calls you 'darling' all the time."

"That's because you're jealous of him."

"Okay. So maybe I am a little bit jealous. He's still a wimp."

"He's in love with me."

"So am I."

"Well, his kisses are a lot warmer than yours."

"I promise you that will change, if I ever get my new body." By this time he was standing next to the sofa, where she still lay with her magazine. "Look," he said, trying to effect a more serious tone, "you owe me the answer to one question."

"What question?"

"I've never asked you this before, but the time has come."

"Okay. What is it?"

"Do you . . . well, you know. Do you feel anything for me? Anything at all?"

"Perhaps."

"Perhaps? What is that supposed to mean?" he pressed, visibly annoyed that she didn't look up from her magazine to answer his question.

"It means perhaps."

"It means you won't say it."

"I might be persuaded."

"What do you want?"

Now she did look up. "I want you to stay out of my date tonight.

Leave me alone, for once, with the man I plan to marry."

"That's coercion."

"You catch on fast—for a ghost. I'll leave the television on for you, okay?"

"I hate that. You know I can't change channels."

"How about a video?"

"Yeah, like last time, I suppose?"

"Okay, so 'Ghost Busters' was a poor choice."

"Slightly."

At that moment there was a knock at the door. "Is that you, Bruce?" she called.

"Yes, darling. It's me."

Grabbing her purse and light wrap, she started for the door. Jason stepped directly in front of her. "You didn't answer my question!" he snapped.

"Not so loud," she scolded. "Bruce is right outside."

"Are you forgetting? That clown can't hear me. Now answer my question!"

"See you tonight," she chuckled, attempting to step around him. The thought of passing through him never occurred to her.

"Answer me now—DAR-LING. Or there will be a threesome on your date for sure."

"That's coercion."

"You catch on fast, for a schoolteacher."

"All right. I do have feelings for you," she replied.

"Well?" he pressed, stepping out of her way.

"Well what?"

"What kind of feelings do you have for me?"

"I think of you as my favorite ghost," she said quickly, scurrying past him to the door. "Bye now. See you in the morning."

"You look lovely tonight, darling," Bruce said, placing Samantha's wrap around her shoulders.

Glancing back at Jason with a mischievous grin, she stepped into the hall and closed the door.

* * * * *

"Her favorite ghost? Is that a morale booster, or what?" Jason fell to the sofa. "Wouldn't you know it, she didn't even turn the television on." Staring at the ceiling, he tried to ignore the empty feeling in the pit of his stomach that always came when Samantha was alone with Bruce. It just didn't seem fair. If it hadn't been for the typo he would have his body now, and could give old Bruce the fight of his life. Jason hated that typo. He hated being a ghost, too. Why couldn't Gus have had the patience to wait one day until his secretary returned?

Jason's moment of self-pity was cut short by the sound of a voice from behind him. "Jason! What are ya' doing here when Sam's out there with Bruce, even as we speak?" It was Gus.

"What am I supposed to do, Gus?" he asked, rising to his feet. "I'm open to suggestions."

"It's not like I don't have big enough problems here. Now ya' let this Bruce guy take over, and ya' don't even put up a fight."

"How am I supposed to fight Bruce? You have to admit he's a little better suited for courting than I am."

"Like I been tellin' ya', Jase, I'll work out the details. In the meantime, you get out there to that car and stay between those two, before things get even more serious."

"Gus, I. . ."

"Cut the talk! Go get in that car!"

"I'm going," Jason scowled. "But you'd better get busy on your end of things, too. I'm losing ground in a hurry to that fast-talking shrink, and if I don't get the body you promised soon. . ."

"I'll take care of my end, Jase. Now I'm tellin ya', get out to that car!"

* * * * *

It was a little after seven-thirty when the black Lexus pulled out of the parking lot. Samantha was almost afraid to look in the back seat. She knew how upset Jason had been when she left the apartment. She had to admit that she had been rough on him, and he really hadn't done a thing to deserve it. His question had, after all, been an honest one. Holding her breath, she glanced over her shoulder. Just as she feared, he was there, grinning mischievously.

"You know what you are?" she snapped. "You're a pain that a

three-pound aspirin can't cure!"

Bruce glanced at Samantha while watching the road out of the corner of his eye. "Are you angry with me, darling?" he puzzled.

"I didn't mean you, Bruce."

"How could you not mean me? There's no one else in the car."

Fidgeting with the leather strap on her purse, she searched for the right words. "Bruce," she struggled, "There's something I've been meaning to tell you."

"Don't do it, Sam," Jason warned. "I can't show myself to him. He'll think you're crazy for sure."

"What is it, my love?" Bruce asked.

"This is not easy for me, Bruce, but you do have a right to know about him."

"About him? There's another man? Oh, Samantha, no wonder you won't marry me!"

"No, Bruce. That's not it at all."

The traffic light ahead turned yellow and Bruce jammed the breaks hard, bringing the car to a jerky stop at the intersection. "Well, if it's not another man, why did you mention 'him?'"

"Well, Bruce, you see he's. . ."

"He's what, Samantha?!"

"There's no easy way to say this, Bruce, so you had better brace yourself. I have a ghost!"

"What?" Bruce yelled, his face red from the sudden rush of blood, and his left eye twitching violently.

"I said, I'm being haunted by a ghost."

"You couldn't leave well enough alone, could you, Sam," Jason lamented. "You've really stirred the hornets now."

Bruce's voice raised an octave. "There's no such thing as ghosts!" he screamed.

"You're wrong, Bruce. I have a ghost, and he is in the back seat right now."

Bruce spun to see an empty back seat. The sound of blaring car horns brought his attention to the traffic light, which had turned green. He jammed the accelerator to the floor. The car lurched forward with screeching tires burning against the cold pavement. At the next block he made a quick right onto a cross street and brought the car to an abrupt stop next to a vacant lot.

"There's no one in the back seat!" he snapped, looking again.

"Oh, he's there all right. Unfortunately, I'm the only one who can see him."

"Samantha, darling, this is so unlike you. It's completely crazy!"

"Crazy or not, the ghost is real. In fact, you're the one who proved how real he is."

"I what?!"

"Where do you think I came up with the information about the soldier in Vietnam?"

"The mess cook?"

"Yes, the mess cook. The reason I knew about him is he told me himself."

"That's preposterous! The man died over twenty years ago."

"That is exactly what I have been trying to tell you, Bruce. That soldier is now a ghost, and he is sitting in the back seat, right behind you."

Bruce looked again at the back seat. "You really believe there's someone there, don't you, Samantha?"

"Come on, you stubborn ghost, help me out here! Do something to prove you're there!"

"Wow, Sam, do you know what you're asking of me? I've never had to prove myself to anyone before."

"Well, you can prove yourself now. Do something!"

Jason spent a moment in heavy thought. "Okay, let's try this. Tell him to write something on a piece of paper and lay it on the seat next to me. I'll read it aloud, and you can tell him what it says."

"That might work."

"You talk to him, and he answers you?" Bruce asked in a daze.

"Yes, and he has an idea on how we can prove to you he's really there. He says for you to write something on a paper and not let me see it."

"Samantha! I'm a psychologist. Psychologists help people understand there are no such things as ghosts. Not vice versa."

"Just do it, Bruce!"

Samantha's tone left no doubt in Bruce's mind that she meant what she said. He decided not to argue. Opening his wallet, he removed a business card. Then, using the pen from his shirt pocket, he scribbled a few words on the back of the card. He was careful not to allow Samantha to see what he had written.

"Tell him to lay it in on the back seat, Sam."

"The ghost says to lay the card on the back seat."

Bruce turned and gave the card a hasty toss.

"It landed upside down. I can't read it unless he turns it over."

"He said the card landed upside down. You'll have to turn it over."

"If he is a ghost as you suggest, he should be able read it like it is."

"Where did this guy learn about ghosts? I can't read it unless he turns it over."

"He says you don't understand ghosts, and insists you turn the card over."

"Of course I don't understand ghosts. They don't exist. However, I will turn the card over just to play the game out."

"Tell him to turn on the overhead light. It's too dark back here to read it."

"He asks for you to turn on the dome light."

"That's it, Samantha! This thing has gone far enough!"

"Turn on the light! NOW!"

Bruce twisted the switch, and the light came on. "Okay, now let's see what excuse your ghost will come up with."

"I read it," Jason laughed. "Boy, is old Bruce going to be in trouble with you for this one."

"Never mind how much trouble Bruce will be in, just tell me what he wrote!"

"Okay, Sam. This is his note. 'Samantha, my love, you seem to be suffering from a severe case of hallucinations. Make an appointment with my secretary. You need my help badly.'"

"Bruce, you pompous jerk!" she snapped. "I am not suffering from hallucinations, and I refuse to call your secretary for an appointment."

The color rushed from Bruce's face. He turned again to search the back seat. All he saw was the card lying there where he had placed it. "It's a trick, darling. You're playing a trick on me, right? Tell me how you did it."

"Hey!" Jason cried. "This is great fun. Let's try another one! Tell him to put his hand behind the seat."

"I'm not pulling any tricks on you, Bruce. There really is a ghost. He asks now that you put a hand behind your seat, where I can't see it."

Beads of perspiration dotted Bruce's forehead. "I'm not sure I want to put my hand back there," he admitted.

"Bruce!"

"All right, Samantha, I'll do it. What now?"

"Have him hold up some fingers, and I'll tell you how many he is holding up."

"The ghost wants you to hold up some fingers. He'll tell me the number."

Staring hard at the empty seat, Bruce gingerly held up all four fingers where he was sure Samantha could not see.

"He is holding up four fingers," Jason said.

"Four fingers."

"Now he is holding up two fingers and his thumb."

"Two fingers and a thumb."

"How crude, now he's shaking his clenched fist at me."

"Bruce! Stop shaking your fist at him. He may be a ghost, but he still has feelings."

Bruce jerked back his hand. "All right, Samantha! I'm not sure what's going on here, but I intend to find out once and for all. So far we've done this your way."

"No, Bruce. We've been doing it the way the ghost has suggested."

"As you wish, darling. But this time we'll do it my way."

Shutting off the engine, he stepped from the car, and without saying a word walked toward a street light several yards away. "Tell your ghost to follow me," he called back.

"I heard him."

"He heard you."

Having reached the street light, Bruce removed the change from his pocket, and held it in his open hand under the light. Speaking to what he considered to be nothing more than the evening air, he said,

"Here ghost, look at the change in my hand." He pocketed the money and returned to the car, where he leaned in the window with a smug expression on his face and said nothing.

"Tell him to brace himself, Sam."

"The ghost wants me to warn you to brace yourself."

"Your little game's over, darling. There's no way you can foil the scheme I've thought up to disprove the ghost."

"Tell him he has seventy-eight cents in change in his right front pocket," Jason said and laughed.

"The ghost says you have seventy-eight cents in change in your right front pocket."

Bruce jerked backward, slamming the back of his head against the window frame. Frantically he searched for the ghost, who suddenly had become quite real. "Where is he? Is he going to hurt me?"

"Calm down, Bruce; the ghost is harmless. Believe me, you're in no danger."

"What does he want? Why is he haunting us?"

"It's a long story, and I promise to explain everything when you've had a chance to calm down."

Samantha slid to the driver's side of the car. "Give me your keys," she said.

"What?" he asked, obviously in a state of shock.

"You're in no condition to drive. Now get in the car. I'm driving us back to my apartment."

Bruce didn't argue, but did as she asked. "Is . . . you know . . . still in the back seat?"

"He's there."

A very confused psychologist never took his eyes off the back seat all the way to the Anderson apartment building.

CHAPTER TEN

"Are you going to invite me in?" Bruce asked, still dazed from his experience.

Samantha opened the door. "Do you think you're calm enough now to discuss things rationally?"

"I think so."

"Well then, by all means, do come in."

Bruce looked utterly dazed. He staggered into the living room and somehow managed to seat himself on the sofa next to Samantha.

"Would you like something to drink?" she asked.

"No, darling, nothing thanks," he managed. "I just need some answers. Is the ghost here now?"

"Sam! If you're bent on doing this thing, then do it right. Explain to the man that I'm not really a ghost."

"He's here, and he wants me to tell you he is not a ghost."

"Not a ghost? I don't understand."

"Neither do I. It's best just to humor him on this one."

"Where is he now?"

Samantha rose from the sofa and walked to the opposite side of the room, near the artificial fireplace. "He's standing right here," she answered, staring at what looked like empty space.

Bruce squinted his eyes, as though it would help him see something. It didn't help. "Are you absolutely certain, darling, we have nothing to fear from him?"

"He's harmless."

"It would be much simpler if your ghost would just show himself to me."

"I'm sorry, Sam. I wish I could, but I don't make the rules."

"He apologizes, but explains he can't do that."

"That's a lie! I'd never apologize to that wimp, even if I had a reason to."

"I accept his apology, but I hope he understands how difficult this is for a man trained to believe in the nonexistence of ghosts."

"You remind me of a horse with blinders. Nothing exists to you unless it bites you on the nose."

"He says he understands."

"Is it too much to ask . . . ?"

"What is it you want, Bruce? Go ahead and ask it."

"I'd like to have just one more demonstration. Perhaps it will dispel all doubt from my mind."

"Absolutely not! I've given him enough proof already."

"The ghost will be glad to oblige," she answered, glaring at Jason.

Bruce pulled a letter from his pocket, which he explained was from one of his clients. "Can your ghost tell me who signed this letter?"

"If he wants me to read the thing he can bring it to me. I'm not going over there."

"You have to understand, Bruce, this is a very stubborn ghost. The only way he'll read it is if you take it to him. He refuses to come to you."

Bruce stood and moved cautiously to where Samantha had indicated Jason was standing. She returned to the couch.

Jason broke out in laughter. "This guy's shaking so badly, I can't begin to read what he's holding in front of me."

"He wants you to hold it steady. He says you're trembling so badly he can't read it."

Bruce was holding the letter with his hand extended as far as he could reach. He wanted to keep the greatest possible distance between himself and the ghost. Using both hands, he managed to hold it a little more steady.

"It's signed by Joyce Ramsey. She is accusing him of grossly overcharging her."

"Joyce Ramsey is complaining you overcharged her," Samantha repeated.

"He is real." Bruce crumpled the letter and crammed it back into his coat pocket. "You really do have a ghost," he said in a somber voice, while falling back to the sofa.

"I'm glad you finally agree on that point, Bruce," she said, tapping his hand with hers.

"Never in my life have I encountered anything of this nature. It certainly makes me wonder about some of the clients I have diagnosed as having overactive imaginations. Perhaps I may have been mistaken."

"Well!" Jason exclaimed in surprise. "I'm impressed. There may be hope for this guy yet."

"Samantha, darling," Bruce said after gathering his thoughts, "there are so many things you must explain to me."

"You're right, Bruce. We definitely need to talk."

Then, beginning with Jason's first appearance on the evening of their dinner date at the Hunter's Cottage, she related the story just the way it happened. She admitted to fainting the first time he walked through a wall, and told of their conversation the following morning. Next, she rehearsed the events that took place in the park one week later, and ended with the night at the Morgans'. All the while, Bruce listened intently.

She was careful to avoid any mention of the ghost courting her, or of Gus.

"There's one thing I don't understand, darling," Bruce said as she concluded. "Why is he haunting you?"

Samantha bit her lip, and pondered whether or not to finish that part of the story.

"Come on, lady. You've gone this far, tell him I'm his rival. Tell him I'm in love with you, too."

She concluded he had the right to know it all. "I hope you're ready for this, Bruce. The ghost doesn't think of himself as haunting me."

"Not haunting you? That's absurd. What else could you call what he's doing but haunting?"

Samantha reached for Bruce's hand, and pulled it to her lap. She smiled warmly, trying to soften the impact of what she was about to tell him. The words came hard. "He thinks he's. . ."

"Yes, darling, go on."

"By all means, Sam! Answer his question."

"He thinks he's courting me."

"Courting you!" Bruce shouted. "Did you say he thinks he's *courting* you?"

"Yes, Bruce. That's exactly what I said."

"You mean I'm in competition with a—ghost?"

"Calm down, Bruce. It's your ring I'm wearing, remember?"

"How can you be courted by a ghost? He can't marry you. Can he?"

"Yes!" Jason shouted. "Just as soon as Gus figures out a way!"

"No, of course not," Samantha answered, ignoring the remark.

"That's not fair!" Jason fumed. "Tell Bruce about Gus trying to get me another body."

"No!" Samantha shouted. "That's as far as I go!"

Bruce was puzzled. "Were you talking to me, darling, or to . . . ?"

"No, Bruce," she said, squeezing his arm. "I wasn't talking to you." She could see this was going to be even more difficult than she had anticipated. "If I'm not looking at you when I say something, just assume I mean the ghost. All right, Bruce?"

"I'll try, but you must admit this whole thing is quite confusing." He pulled her hand to his chest, and looked at her with boyish eyes. "Do you still plan on marrying me, darling?"

"Yes, Bruce. Nothing's changed between us."

"What about after that? Will the ghost still be . . . ?"

"Haunting us?"

"Is that what you think of him as doing, even though he denies it?"

"I do, and no, he won't be haunting us any longer after we're married. He's given me his word."

Bruce removed the handkerchief from his coat pocket and wiped his brow. "How about our dating? Have we been alone, or has he been there, too?"

"That's a major point of contention between this stubborn ghost and me," she answered, scowling at Jason. "He often refuses to honor my privacy when it comes to you, Bruce."

"Sam, I know you won't believe me, but I wasn't planning on going along on your date tonight."

"You're right, I don't believe you."

"Do you mean me?"

"No, Bruce. I wasn't looking at you, was I?"

"Gus talked me into it. Tonight was his idea."

"Gus talked you into it? Why, pray tell, did he do that?"

"He says I have to look out for my interests. I can't let you go falling for Bruce without a fight. We have to get destiny back on its designed course."

"Darling! Who is Gus?"

"No one important, Bruce. He is just someone the ghost has dreamed up."

"You know perfectly well Gus is real," Jason argued.

"Will you just shut up about Gus?"

"Who are you talking to, darling? Me, or the ghost?"

"That's it!" she snapped, jumping to her feet. "I've had about all I can stand of either of you for one night! I'd like you both to leave, now!"

"I think she means it, Bruce. Too bad you can't hear me; I'd tell you how she tried to shoot me once."

"That's a lie. You know as well as I do that gun wouldn't shoot."

"Gun, what gun?"

"Never mind, Bruce," she shouted, moving quickly to the door and flinging it open. "Good night to both of you!"

"May I call you tomorrow, darling?"

"Of course," she said with a light good night kiss. "Believe me, nothing has changed between us."

Samantha closed the door and leaned hard against it. With a big sigh, she let her mind drift backward to a time when there was no such thing as ghosts. Life was so much simpler back then.

CHAPTER ELEVEN

Samantha smiled as she watched her twenty-one squirming pupils. Their eyes were fixed keenly on the clock mounted over the large world map on the east classroom wall. Once every second the thin black hand clicked forward a fraction of an inch. Then, with tormenting precision, it would fall back half the distance. At last, the hand agonized its way to the twelve and, to the delight of all, the final bell rang out.

"Class dismissed." Before the words had escaped Samantha's lips the room was in turmoil, with students fighting to be first through the door.

With the last student gone, Samantha glanced at the mass of work papers on her desk. Try as she might, she just couldn't concentrate on them. Instead, her thoughts drifted to the ghost, and to the changes that had come into her life because of him. He had not been around since last Friday night, when Bruce learned of him.

Bruce, on the other hand, had called several times during the week. On Wednesday evening, she had gone to his place for a nice dinner.

She was surprised at how well he was handling the ghost thing, except for one aggravating problem. He had shifted his "marry me now" campaign into high gear. He argued that it would get rid of the ghost problem, once and for all. His constant pressure was beginning to annoy her.

Perhaps he was right, though. She was fond of Bruce, and marrying him would be one solution to the problem. Then too, the lifestyle he offered was always a temptation.

Fumbling through the pile of work on her desk, she picked up a stack of test papers that were ready for grading. Then she noticed him.

Sitting in a fifth-grader's chair at the back of the room was her favorite ghost. He looked so ridiculous sitting in that little chair that she couldn't keep from laughing.

"What's so funny?" he asked indignantly.

"If you don't know, I can never tell you. What are you doing here, anyway?"

"I have my reasons," he said, making sure to walk around everything in his way as he approached the desk. He knew how upset she could get when he walked through something.

"What kind of stuff are you teaching these kids nowadays? I'll swear, in my day, we didn't learn typing until high school."

"How long have you been here, anyway?"

"About half an hour. You didn't notice me for all the kids."

"Well," she explained, "the world has come a long way since you were in school. These kids need to know things you never dreamed of during your lifetime. They have to learn typing at an early age because they need to use computers."

He sat on the edge of the desk and leaned toward her. "I'll tell you something else that's changed, too, lady. In my day, we didn't have teachers half as pretty as the one these kids are blessed with."

"Well, thank you," she beamed. "What a nice compliment."

"For a ghost, you mean?"

"I didn't say that. Not this time, anyway."

"You're in a good mood today, Sam. Any particular reason?"

"It's none of your business why I'm in a good mood." Then she thought of something she hadn't before. She knew he could do strange things like walking through walls, but what about her thoughts? Could he know what she had just been thinking about Bruce?

"Can you read my thoughts?" she asked nervously.

"Can I do what?"

"I just asked if you have a way of knowing what I'm thinking."

"Why?" he frowned. "Have you been thinking bad things about me again?"

"Don't be silly, I wouldn't do that. But can you . . . read my thoughts, I mean?"

"Of course I can't read your thoughts. Why would you ever think a thing like that?"

"Oh," she beamed.

"Does that make you happy, knowing I can't read your thoughts?"

"Yes. It does. I don't think I would want you around if you could do that."

"Can I take that to mean you do want me around, the way I really am?"

"I have to admit, I am getting used to you. It's not so bad having you around, I guess."

"I like it when you're in a good mood, Sam, but you never told me what brought it on."

"I suppose I'm in a good mood," she said, "just because it's a nice day."

"By the way," he asked, "where is it?"

"Where is what, you big nut?"

"The apple, of course."

"The apple?"

"Yeah. In my day, we brought an apple for the teacher. So where's your apple?"

"Is that all you're here for, to give me a hard time?"

"No, as a matter of fact it's not. Actually, I'm here for a very special reason. One I think you're going to like."

"You've come to tell me you've found someone else to haunt and you're going to set me free, right?"

"Sam!"

"I'm sorry," she laughed. "You left yourself wide open, and I just couldn't resist. Forgive me?"

"I forgive you."

"Now the truth. What am I going to like about your being here?"

The warmth of his smile told her something special was about to happen, but she didn't know what. "Look behind you, Sam," he said.

"Look behind me?"

"Yeah, that's what I said, look behind you."

Slowly, she turned around. If given a thousand chances, she would never have guessed what, or rather who, she would see there.

"GRANDAD!" she squealed in delight. "IS IT REALLY YOU?"

"Yes, child, it's me all right."

Springing from her chair without thinking, she rushed to him. "NO, SAM!" he cried, extending his hand to stop her. His warning was too late. She rushed headlong to him, only to slide through his image like sunlight through a window.

"I'm sorry, Sam," he sadly exclaimed. "I tried to stop you."

"It's okay, Grandad," she said, regaining her composure. "At least I can see you. You look just great."

"I'll bet I do look better than the last time you saw me."

"That's not funny!" she scolded, remembering his lifeless body in that cold metal coffin.

"If you think I look good like this, you should see the way I *really* look now."

"I don't understand."

"You see me like you remember me, when I was mortal. It's the only way you would recognize me. To you, I look eighty years old. If you could see me the way I really look now, about like age twenty-five, you wouldn't even know me."

"How does that kind of thing work, Grandad?"

"It's beyond me, child. I just know it does work, and that's enough for now."

"Why do you say it's enough for now?"

"Because I just keep learning. In time, I'm sure I'll understand this, too."

"You keep learning?"

"I learn something new every day."

"What about Grandma? Does she look young?"

"She's a fox, just like the teenage girl I married in 1916."

"Are the two of you still together?"

"Of course we're together! We were covered by one of Gus's special contracts, too."

"Sorry, Grandad. I just don't understand about those special contracts, or about how things are where you live now."

"We're happier than we've ever been, Sam. Life is great on this side, especially if you have the right person to share it with. Like your grandmother and I have each other."

Samantha was bubbling with excitement. "Why are you here?

How long will you stay? Can I see Grandma, too?"

"Whoa, child! Slow up a bit! You're too full of questions. Let's take one at a time."

"He's here on a temporary pass," Jason explained. "Gus worked it all out with the higher authorities."

"Temporary pass? What's a temporary pass?" she asked.

"Well, he's here on a one-time assignment as my character reference."

"A character reference?"

"Jason," the grandfather interrupted, "why don't you let me handle this. My granddaughter and I should have this brief moment just for the two of us, don't you agree?"

Jason wanted to protest. He wished he could be there to represent his own case. He realized, however, that Grandfather Collens was right. Grumbling something neither one understood, he walked through the wall to the outside schoolyard.

"I hate it when he does that, Grandad. Why is he haunting me, and what did he mean when he called you his character reference?"

"I'll try to answer all your questions, Sam, but let's take them one at a time. Where do you want to start?"

Her heart raced with excitement as she looked into the gentle eyes of this man she loved so dearly. She wanted this moment to last. "How long can you stay, Grandad?"

"Not long, child. Jason was right about the temporary pass."

"Tell me about yourself, and Grandma. What are things like for the two of you now?"

"I'm a little limited in what they let me say about things like that. You're not supposed to know too much about it until you get there yourself."

"Can you tell me anything at all?"

"About all I can say is that Sally and I are very happy."

"You say you don't really look like I'm seeing you now. You actually look younger?"

"That's right, child."

"Can I see you as you really are?"

"Nope. It's against the rules. You have to see me the way you remember me."

"I'm confused," she replied. "When I look at . . . you know. He looks younger to me now than he could have been when he died."

"Are you talking about Jason?"

"Yes."

"Why not call him by his name?"

"I . . . have a hard time with that one."

"Give the lad a chance, child; he's a fine man. To answer your question, you see him like he really is because you never met him in his mortal life. You have no memory of what he looked like, so that rule doesn't apply with him."

"Is that the real reason you're here, to tell me about him?"

The two had become so involved in conversation that they both failed to hear the door open as Bruce entered the room. "Samantha, my dear," he asked. "Who are you talking to? Is your ghost here now?"

Caught completely off guard by his unexpected visit, Samantha could manage no more than a stuttered question. "Bruce? Wha— what are you doing here?"

"I wanted to be with you, darling. I thought we might go some- where."

"Why didn't you call?"

"Must I always call before I come to see you?"

Samantha glanced quickly back to her grandfather, fearing he might have gone. Her heart jumped in relief when she saw he was still there. "No, Bruce, of course you don't have to call first," she replied, her mind racing for a solution to this sudden dilemma.

"Use your head, Sam." It was Jason who spoke. "Tell him you have to use the girls' room. I doubt if even Bruce would follow you in there."

"Yes, of course! The girls' room! Wait here, Bruce, I need to make a visit to the girls' room. I'll only be a few minutes."

"You're acting strange, Samantha. That ghost is here, isn't he?"

"Bruce, if you tell me I'm acting strange once more. . . "

"Sorry, darling," he said, searching the room. "I'll wait here for you, but I hope I'm alone."

Jason and Grandfather Collens were already there when Samantha rushed into the rest room. "This is crazy!" she snapped at

Jason, after assuring herself that the room was not already in use. "You shouldn't be in here."

"Do you have a better idea?" he asked. She didn't have to answer. Her look told him he had better make a fast exit. He did.

"I'm sorry, Grandad. I had no idea Bruce would show up at the school. He seldom does that."

"That's okay, child. I understand how awkward this can be. That's precisely why it is only done on a limited basis. I suppose we should get on with the real reason I am here."

"To tell me why I'm being haunted?"

"He's not really haunting you, sweetheart."

"He says he is courting me."

"Well, that's a strange way to word it, but he's right. That's about what he's doing. His destiny is linked to yours. Gus's typo on your special contract threw everything out of kilter. Jason should be a young man in his prime right now. Then he could have courted you properly. Unfortunately, under the circumstances, he has to make do with what he has."

"But Grandad, he's a ghost. I couldn't marry a ghost, even if I wanted to."

"That, my dear, is Gus's problem. Believe me, he'll work it out. He's the biggest horse trader I've ever known, and in my lifetime I came across plenty of talented horse traders."

"What about Bruce?"

"Are you in love with him, child?"

"I'm very fond of him."

"That's not what I asked! Are you in love with him?"

"I—don't think so."

"Marrying Bruce would be a mistake. Take my word for it, Jason is the right one for you. Leave it to Gus to work out the details, child."

"Even if Gus did work something out, what would become of Bruce? Does he have a special contract with someone else?"

"I doubt he has a contract like yours, Sam. This kind of contract is issued only on a special basis, which I don't understand yet."

"I would never want to hurt Bruce. He's a fine man, and he has always been good to me."

"I tell you what, child. You could have Jason ask Gus about it. Gus is in charge of the department that handles all special contracts. He'd know about Bruce for sure."

Then, without warning, Grandfather Collens turned to the wall on Samantha's right and said, "We had to have some privacy. I didn't pick this place; it was Jason's idea."

"Grandad," Samantha said, looking at the empty space he was facing, "why are you talking to that wall? Have I missed something here?"

"Oh, sorry, dear," he answered with a chuckle. "I wasn't talking to the wall. I was talking to your grandmother."

"Grandma is here?!" Samantha shouted. "Where is she?"

"Standing right next to you, Sam. She wanted to know why we're in the ladies' room."

"Please, Grandad, let me see her, too!"

"Look in the mirror, child."

Believing that he meant a reflection of her grandmother would somehow show up in the mirror, Samantha quickly looked. To her disappointment, she saw the images of only herself and her grandfather.

"I can't see her, Grandad. Not even in the mirror."

"I know that, it's against the rules. She doesn't have a pass."

"But you said if I looked in the mirror . . . "

"You see yourself, don't you, girl?"

"Of course."

"Well then, you see Sally."

"You mean we look alike?"

"The two of you are the spitting image of each other. I even have a hard time telling you apart."

"Grandma, can you hear me?"

"Of course she can hear you, child."

"I love you, Grandma. I miss you, too."

"She says she loves you, but she thinks it's her apple pies you miss the most."

Samantha laughed through eyes filling with happy tears. What wonderful memories of Grandma's apple pies she had!

"I already told her that, Sally."

"What did she say, Grandad?"

"She asked me to tell you she doesn't like that Bruce fellow, and wants you to stick with Jason."

"This isn't fair. You're ganging up on me."

"We love you, child. We want you to be as happy as we are. We know you can't do that with Bruce."

"Why can't I be happy with Bruce? He's a good man, and he treats me like a lady—most of the time."

"He may be a good man, child, but destiny has you and Jason teamed up, not you and Bruce."

"I just can't understand that, Grandad."

"Take my word for it, Sam, I know what I'm talking about. Never mess around with something that's been destined."

"Does this destiny thing mean I don't have the right to make my own choice?"

"Of course not, child. The final choice is yours alone."

"Even if that choice is not the one I'm told destiny wants me to make?"

"Even then, the choice is yours."

Tears were flowing freely down her face by this time. She grew quiet, studying the face of her beloved grandfather, and pondered the things he had told her. Without his saying a word, she somehow knew the time had come for him to leave. "I love you, Grandad." She had to choke out the words.

"I love you too, child, but my time's up now."

"I know."

"Your grandmother has dinner waiting for me, Sam. You should remember how upset she gets if everyone is not there when she puts it on the table."

"I remember, Grandad," she sobbed. "Will I see you again?"

"Of course you'll see me again! But, most likely, not like this. My pass was good only for one quick visit, and I doubt if I will ever get another one. Remember what I have told you, child. You won't regret waiting until Gus figures things out." He smiled, and turned to leave.

"Wait!" she cried. "I want to ask you one more question."

"Yes, Sam?" he asked, turning to face her again.

"Why did you give me that worthless gun? You could have

caused me to get hurt if I had ever really needed it."

"Your grandmother has already made me pay dearly for that one. I just thought you would never need it. Forgive me?"

"I forgive you, Grandad. Be seeing you."

"Goodbye, child," he said, tears in his own eyes. Then, turning, he stepped into the mirror. He and his reflection seemed to mold together, and then both images vanished.

Samantha dried her eyes, washed her face, and walked slowly back to the classroom. Peering through the small window in the door, she broke into laughter. There, sitting side by side in the little chairs were two figures. One a man, the other a ghost. It was hard to tell which one looked the most worried.

CHAPTER TWELVE

Samantha opened the door and entered the classroom laughing. "Do you two know how ridiculous you look?" she asked.

"Then I was right," Bruce snapped. "The ghost is here, isn't he?"

"He is. Sitting in the chair to your left, in fact."

Bruce jumped to his feet and moved quickly to Samantha's side. "I thought he was here from the way you were acting when I first arrived. What does he want this time?"

"He brought someone to see me, someone very special." Her face shone with excitement as she remembered. "I just talked with my grandad. I was talking to him when you walked in on us earlier."

Bruce went pale and fell back to his chair. "You mean, you have two ghosts haunting you now?"

"Bruce Vincent! Don't you ever call my grandfather a ghost!"

Jason snickered. "It figures—you think of me as a ghost, but you don't think of your grandfather as one. What's the difference, Sam?"

"I don't know what the difference is. All I know is, I can't think of Grandad like that."

"Did the two of you have a good talk?"

"It was wonderful," she sighed. "Thank you for bringing him."

"It was his idea, not mine. I have to admit, though, I appreciate all the help I can get. Did he put in a good word for me?"

"He did at that."

"Samantha, darling," Bruce said, standing again and trying to keep her between him and where he thought the ghost must be, "I find this all very confusing."

"What's confusing, Bruce?"

"Listening to this one-sided conversation. You have no idea what it's like."

"That's where you're wrong. I know exactly what it's like. I just went through the same thing myself, not five minutes ago."

She couldn't help laughing at the blank looks on their faces. "I'm sorry for laughing," she said. "It's just that sometimes I find the two of you so amusing."

"I'm glad we could make your day, Sam," Jason huffed, "but are you going to explain yourself or not?"

"Okay," she said, wiping her eyes with a tissue from the box on her desk. "I'll explain. While I was talking to Grandad, my grandmother was there, too."

"Your grandmother?" the two asked simultaneously.

"Yes, my grandmother. Just like you, Bruce, I had to depend on a translator. I could neither see nor hear her. It was funny watching Grandad talk to her, like he was talking to the air. So you see, Bruce, I do know how you feel."

"It's humiliating, to say the least," he replied.

"Oh, I don't know. I thought it was kind of fun. How many people ever have that happen to them?"

"I simply cannot see why you call that fun. I hate it, and I wish you'd ask the ghost to leave. I'd like to be alone with you tonight."

"Why should I have to leave?" Jason protested. "I was here first! If anyone leaves, it should be the wimp!"

"Enough of this!" Samantha cried. "I'll decide who I want to leave, and who I want to stay. You two are acting like my pupils. Why can't you learn to get along with each other?"

"I just don't like that ghost hanging around you, Samantha."

"Yeah, and I don't like you either, pickle face!"

"Fine," she said matter-of-factly. "Either or both of you can leave if you like. As for me, I'm in the mood for some fun tonight."

"Yes, darling," Bruce was quick to say. "I thought I would take you home so you could change. Then perhaps we could take in a play, or maybe even the opera."

"I have a better idea," she said, gathering up the books and papers from her desk. "Give me the keys to your car. I'll drive."

"Where on earth are we going?" Bruce asked as the two made their way to his car. Jason was not far behind.

"You'll see when we get there," she answered. The three got in the car and she pulled it out of the parking lot, making a left turn at the street.

"This is not the way to your apartment," Bruce complained.

"You're right, it's not. We always do exactly what you want, Bruce. Tonight it's my turn. This time, we do it my way."

"And what, pray tell, might that be, darling?"

"For starters," she chuckled, "I'm hungry for a Big Mac and a large order of fries."

"You expect me to eat in a fast-food restaurant?"

"No, Bruce," she answered. "If you want to wait in the car while I eat, it's okay with me."

Jason laughed. "I told you this guy is a wimp, didn't I, Sam?"

"Couldn't we eat at a more respectable place, darling?"

"If you want to marry me, Bruce, you had better learn one thing right now. McDonald's comes with this lady; I'm hooked on their french fries."

Bruce sulked in silence as she drove to the nearest McDonald's, where she wheeled into a parking space. "Are you coming or not?" she called, halfway to the entrance.

Disgustedly, Bruce opened his door and stepped out. "Is that pesky ghost still with us?"

"Tell that wimp not to call me pesky!"

"He's here."

"Well, I'm not paying for his hamburger."

"May I help you?" a little gray-haired woman asked cheerfully from behind the counter.

"I'll have a Big Mac, a large order of fries, and a chocolate shake," Samantha replied cheerfully.

"And you, sir? What will you have this evening?"

"Just get me a glass of water."

"Give the old stick-in-the-mud the same thing I'm having," Samantha said. "He thinks he's having to pay for it, that's why he's so cheap. It's okay, Bruce. This is my treat."

"Yes ma'am," the little lady smiled, turning to fill the order.

"Why did you say that, Samantha? You know perfectly well I'm not cheap."

"I notice you didn't deny being a stick-in-the-mud."

"That'll be $8.25," the little lady said, placing part of the order on a tray. "You can get started on your fries and shakes. It'll be a couple of minutes on the Big Macs. I'll bring them out as soon as they're ready."

Over Bruce's objection, Samantha handed her a crisp ten-dollar bill. "I'll trust him with the change," she said, crossing the aisle to pick up the straws, catsup, and napkins.

Bruce grabbed the change, then followed. "Why do they call this a fast-food place?" he grumbled. "If you have to wait for the main part of the order to be brought out, it doesn't seem like fast food to me."

"Can't you just relax for once in your life? So we have to wait two minutes for the burgers."

"Over here!" Jason called from a table where he was already seated.

"This way, Bruce," Samantha echoed. "Jason has already picked out a table, in the non-smoking section."

"Oh, no!" Bruce moaned, seeing the table they were headed for. "Do we have to sit here?" he protested. Hanging on the wall, over the table, was a larger-than-life Ronald McDonald. "What if someone I know sees me sitting under that thing?"

"It's all right, Bruce. I really don't think Ronald would mind that much."

"At least I can take comfort in the thought that no one I know would come to a place like this, so I'm reasonably safe."

"Oh!" Samantha exclaimed, seeing Jason with food of his own. "I see you've already been served. Was Gus here?"

"He was," Jason answered.

"Gus?" Bruce asked, looking bewildered. "There's that name again."

"Never mind, Bruce. It's hard to explain. Just let it go, okay?"

"Does the ghost eat?" he wanted to know.

"Not the same things as us, but yes, he does eat. Well, I'll be," she gasped, looking closely at what Jason was eating. "Why does your order look so much like a Big Mac and McDonald's fries?"

"Do you know who Ray Kroc is?" Jason asked, trying to sound very knowledgeable.

"Of course I know who Ray Kroc is. He was the founder of the McDonald's chain."

"Well, to put it in words you like to use, he's a ghost now, too."

"Are you kidding me? They have McDonald's over there?"

"Yep, and lucky for me they do. I got hooked on these fries over thirty years ago. I'd sure hate to do without them."

"What are you two talking about now, darling?"

Samantha dipped a fry in catsup and whisked it into her mouth. "I just learned there's a ghost version of McDonald's," she answered.

"I should have guessed," he shrugged.

Suddenly a strange thought crossed Samantha's mind, causing her to laugh out loud. "I was wondering," she asked Jason, "you haven't, by chance, seen Elvis, have you?"

"No," he chuckled, sampling one of his own fries. "Elvis I haven't seen. In fact, I suspect he's still on your side hiding out someplace."

Just as the hamburgers were being delivered, a man who had been seated across the room rose and walked to their table. "Bruce, old fellow," he said. "Fancy seeing you here."

Bruce glanced up, and suddenly choked on the tiny bite of fry he had just sampled. "Professor Weston," he coughed.

Samantha studied the man. He was an older, fully-bearded gentleman in a gray plaid suit and striped tie.

"What are you doing here, sir?" Bruce asked after managing to get the fry down.

"I eat here all the time," the old gentleman answered. "Somehow, though, I would never have expected to see you here. Are you going to introduce me to this beautiful young lady?"

"Oh yes, Professor," Bruce stumbled. "This is Samantha. Samantha, this is Michael Weston. He was my favorite professor of psychology."

"I'm happy to meet you, Professor," she smiled. "You did a good job with Bruce. He is an outstanding psychologist now."

"Charmed, my dear," the professor answered with a kiss to her hand. "As for Bruce here, I'm sure he does well in his profession. I want to know, though . . . is he still as stuffy as he used to be?"

"Yes!" Jason laughed, though it went unheeded by the only person who heard him.

"He has his moments," Samantha replied. "Don't be surprised at his taste for McDonald's, though. He brings me here often."

Bruce sank deeper into his seat.

"Glad to hear it," the professor chuckled. "Bruce, old chap, there may be hope for you yet. By the look of the ring on this young woman's finger, I'd say you were a pretty lucky fellow."

"We're engaged to be married, Professor, if that's what you had in mind."

"When's the date? Am I invited to the wedding?"

Bruce didn't answer, but looked boyishly at Samantha, who smiled and spoke for him. "We haven't set the exact date yet, Professor Weston. I assure you, however, when we do you will be at the top of our guest list."

"Splendid, my dear. I must say, I never expected Bruce to show such fine taste in his bride. It leaves one with a greater feeling of hope for this new generation."

"Why, thank you, Professor," she beamed.

The professor glanced at his watch. "Oh dear," he exclaimed. "I'm late for a staff meeting. It really was a pleasure meeting you, Samantha. It was good seeing you again too, Bruce, especially at McDonald's. It seems your taste in the fairer sex, and in restaurants, has improved immensely."

"How embarrassing," Bruce grumbled as the old gentleman walked away.

"Nonsense," Samantha said. "He was delightful, and he was right about you. You really do need to lighten up."

"That was an all-right guy," Jason observed. "He must not be much of a teacher, though. If Bruce is an example of what he turns out, that is."

A few minutes later, as Samantha was finishing the last bite of her burger, her face lit up. "You know what I want to do next?" she asked.

"I can't possibly imagine," Bruce scowled.

"I want to play miniature golf."

"Samantha!" Bruce protested. "That's a children's game."

"Sounds like great fun to me," Jason added. "I used to be great at it. Back when I could hold a club, I mean."

"You're right, Bruce," she agreed. "It is a children's game; and since I'm a child at heart, I want to play a round."

Bruce folded his arms tightly and extended a lower lip. "I refuse to be a part of anything so childish," he grumped.

Twenty minutes later the threesome stepped up to the first hole. Samantha spotted her ball, and in one swing had it on the green near the bottom of the raised mound that surrounded the cup.

Bruce followed with no attempt to hide his displeasure. His ball shot up the side of the inclined hill, and landed in the grass outside the playing area.

"My turn," Jason called.

"Where did you get the club and ball?" Samantha asked.

Bruce shook his head in disgust. "He has a club and ball? I don't believe this."

"Bruce!" she scolded. "He has the right to some fun, the same as we do. Where did you get the club and ball?" she asked again.

"From Gus, where else? He's a big golf nut on his side. I don't mean miniature golf, I mean out on the big green. He tells me he's won several tournaments over there."

"Well, hit the ball!" Samantha exclaimed. "We don't want to be on this one hole all night, do we?"

"I warn you, Sam. I'm good at this game."

"Just hit the ball, hot shot."

"What's he doing?" Bruce asked impatiently.

"He's hitting the. . . Well, I'll be!"

"What happened, darling?"

"He got a hole in one!"

"I told you I was good, didn't I?"

"All right," she accused, "own up to it. You have some kind of ghostly power over the ball, right?"

"Sam! I don't have strange powers of any kind. I'm just good at this game, and that's all there is to it."

"Is he cheating, my dear?"

"No, Bruce, I don't think he is."

Samantha finished the hole in three strokes; Bruce made it in six. At the finish of the eighteenth and final hole, the score was fifty-four strokes for Jason and seventy-one strokes for Samantha. Bruce quit counting on the sixth hole at one hundred strokes.

"This has been a great evening," Samantha said as they turned in their clubs.

Jason agreed.

"I think we should call it a night," Bruce suggested, obviously bored.

"No way!" Samantha objected. "We have two more things to do to make the evening perfect. Next, we ride the roller coaster."

Bruce's look of boredom changed to an expression of panic. "I—I have never been on a roller coaster in my life," he managed. "Please, darling, don't ask me to do that."

"I'll ride it with you, Sam!" Jason shouted. "I used to ride one back in the forties at Long Beach, California. It was an old wooden rig that went out over the ocean. Boy, how I loved that ride."

"For crying out loud, Bruce, it's only a ride. Even the ghost is willing to do it."

"Yes, my dear, but you must admit, he has less to lose than I do."

"Then you can wait for us on the ground. Come on, my ghostly friend, we are going to have the ride of our life."

Samantha broke into a run toward the roller coaster entrance that was located a short distance from the miniature golf course. Jason was already waiting for her when she reached the ticket booth.

A moment later Bruce caught up, huffing and puffing after his short jaunt. "Make it tickets for two," he gasped, not wanting to be outdone by a ghost.

Bruce and Samantha strapped themselves tightly into the front car. Jason managed to find an unoccupied seat right behind them. Samantha glanced back at him. "You can't strap in, can you?" She seemed genuinely concerned.

Jason shook with laughter. "Do you really think it will matter if I fall out of the darn thing?"

The coaster lunged forward with a sharp jerk and began its long, steep climb to the top of the track. Samantha beamed with anticipation; Bruce looked sick.

As the car neared the top of the incline, Samantha savored the excitement of the moment, looking at the star-filled sky before her. The clanking of the wheels passing over the cross ties, combined with the screams of some teenage girls in the back cars, added to the thrill. The first car peaked the crest, leveled off, and began moving downward. Soon the bright city lights appeared as the car tilted low enough for the horizon to come into view. At last, the tracks appeared below. They seemed to drop straight downward toward a banking turn nearly the length of a football field away. Bruce's hands clutched the rail in near panic.

The last car cleared the crest, slipping free from the mechanism that had powered it upward. Bursting into an accelerated plunge, the coaster shot downward. Two screams rang loudly from the front car. Samantha screamed in delight. Bruce screamed in terror.

Jason laughed so hard it hurt.

Twenty minutes passed before Bruce could get up from the bench where he had collapsed at the end of the ride. When at last he could speak, his only comment was, "I don't feel well."

By the time they reached the car, his color had almost returned. "Can we go home now?" he begged.

Samantha started the engine. "Not until you take me to Swensen's for a hot fudge sundae."

"No!" he protested. "Enough is enough. I will not be seen in another of those places tonight. You can forget the hot fudge sundae!"

"Two hot fudge sundaes," Samantha said cheerfully to the attractive young waitress. "Load them down with extra nuts, use lots of whipped cream, and don't forget the cherry."

Looking across the table at Jason, Samantha was shocked to see that he already had his dessert—a slice of apple pie topped with vanilla ice cream. "How does Gus do it?" she asked. "How does he manage to get here, and then vanish so quickly? You'd think I would see him sometime, wouldn't you?"

"Gus didn't come this time, Sam. Your grandmother brought this to me."

"What did he say now, darling?"

"Never mind, Bruce. You wouldn't believe me anyway."

"Thanks for being a good sport tonight, Bruce," Samantha said, with the three of them back at her apartment. "I can't remember the last time I had so much fun."

"I hope you don't expect this kind of thing too often from me, darling."

"No, Bruce. It's just not you, is it? We have a lot of adjusting to do before we can make a good marriage for ourselves, don't you think?"

"I suppose so, my dear. But I offer you much more in life than children's games, roller coasters, and ice cream."

Jason, too, was caught up in the excitement of the moment. He wanted some more fun that evening. "Sam," he said, "I've never tried haunting anyone before. Why don't you tell me where old Bruce lives, so I can give it a shot? It could be fun, at that."

Samantha looked at Bruce and toyed with whether or not to tell him what Jason had said. She couldn't resist. "You want to know where Bruce lives so you can haunt him awhile, instead of me?" she giggled.

Bruce's face twisted into a look of horror. "Please, Sam, don't tell him where I live!"

"He could follow you home anyway, Bruce."

"I don't want him haunting me. It's bad enough that he interferes with our dates."

"Where does he live, Sam?"

"He lives in a very large house about ten miles north of here."

"What's the address?"

"6834 North Pine Tree Lane," Samantha answered with a wink.

"I'll never be able to sleep tonight. Why did you have to tell him that?"

"When will you ever learn, Bruce? The ghost is harmless."

"Why does he want to know where I live?"

"Good night, Bruce," she said, giving him a gentle push toward the door. "And good night to you, too, my favorite ghost. Thanks to both of you for a great evening. Right now, however, this school-teacher needs some beauty sleep."

CHAPTER THIRTEEN

Bruce crossed the parking lot mumbling to himself and glancing sharply in the direction of any nearby shadow that happened to move. He hated this neighborhood, and always expected a mugger to leap out at him from the shadows or from behind some bush. In the dark he failed to notice the empty can until an unintentional kick sent it tumbling wildly across the pavement. With a shriek, he bounded for his car and fumbled with his key ring, trying to find the switch on the remote door lock and alarm cutoff. After what seemed an incredibly long time, he wrenched the door open and scurried inside. Within seconds the car was zooming out of the parking lot.

Once safely inside the locked car and on his way home, he breathed a sigh of relief and relaxed. Suddenly, his attention shot to the space next to him. Cautiously, he reached across to feel the empty seat with his hand. "Why did she give that ghost my address?" he questioned aloud.

"I'm here," Jason laughed, knowing all the while his words were unheard.

Bruce retracted his hand, but kept watch on the seat out of the corner of his eye.

"I thought haunting you would be kind of fun, Bruce, but it's not working out that way. You're too much of a bore. I think I'll run on ahead and take a look at that big house of yours. What was that address again? Oh yes, 6834 North Pine Tree Lane. I wish you could hear me. I'll bet you'd never be able to sleep tonight if you knew for sure I was around. Oh, well. Take your time, wimp. I'll see you later."

"So this is my big competition," Jason said, looking over Bruce's house. "It doesn't look so great to me. It sort of reminds me of something out of the Herman Munster TV show. It's exactly what I would have expected the old boy to live in. I have to admit, though, he does have a few bucks tied up in the place."

Wanting to get a closer look at the house, he walked toward the front door, when he noticed something strange. *That's odd*, he thought. *I could have sworn I saw a light moving inside. I'd better check this out.*

Quickly, he slipped through the door into the entryway. Once inside, he was startled to hear the sound of muffled voices. *What's going on here?* he puzzled.

Stepping into the living room, he soon discovered the answer to his own question. There he found two men in ski masks loading a giant-screen television set onto a furniture dolly. Both were armed with large-caliber pistols and appeared to be very dangerous.

I've got to warn Bruce! Jason reasoned. *He could be shot if he comes in the house with these bozos here. But how can I warn him? He can't hear me. Maybe Sam can think of something.*

"Sam, wake up!" he shouted, standing next to her bed.

"What's going on?" she asked, still half asleep.

"Get up quick, we have a big problem!"

"You're in my bedroom! I told you never to come in here again!"

"Sam! Shut up for once, and listen to me!"

The urgency in his voice told her something was wrong. "Wait in the other room," she ordered. "I'll be right there."

"There's no time for that. Get your robe on; I won't look!"

"What on earth is the matter?" she asked, throwing on her robe.

"It's Bruce. He's in big trouble. We have to find a way to help him!"

"Calm down, Jason. Tell me slowly, what kind of trouble is Bruce in?"

"His house is being robbed by two dangerous-looking men with guns."

"How could you possibly know that?"

"I was just there, Sam!"

"How fast can you travel, anyway?"

"Sam! There's no time to explain now, just take my word for it! Bruce is in big trouble. If he walks in on those guys. . ."

"What can I do?!"

"Call the police!"

"How am I going to make them believe me? I can't tell them I was warned by a ghost."

"You've got to do something, Sam. If Bruce walks into that house, you just might have another ghost haunting you."

"Wait!" she exclaimed. "Bruce has a mobile phone in his car!" Throwing open the top dresser drawer, she fumbled through the contents until she found what she was looking for—a little red address book. Quickly, she searched the pages. "I know he gave me that number. I have it here somewhere."

"Keep looking, Sam. I'm going to check on Bruce. I'll be back in a bit."

Bruce was just rounding the corner a block from his house. "Stop!" Jason screamed. "Don't go near that house!"

"That's strange," Bruce muttered. "I have the strongest feeling I shouldn't go home right now."

"Bruce! It's not just a feeling, it's real. Turn around!"

"I wonder why people have feelings like this at times? Who knows? It might be the ghost playing a trick on me."

"It's no trick, Bruce! Stop the car!"

"Look, you pesky ghost, if it is you, I just want you to know I'm not afraid of you."

"Bruce, you idiot! If you can sense what I am saying, listen to your senses. Don't go in that house!"

"Samantha told me you're harmless, and I believe her. You might as well go haunt someone else."

Bruce turned the car into his driveway and pressed the garage door opener just as his mobile phone rang.

"Hurry, Sam!" Jason screamed, back at her side again. "He's about to pull his car into the garage!"

"Bruce!" she yelled into the phone. "Don't go in the house!"

"Samantha, darling. What's this all about?"

"There are two armed men in your house! You could be shot!"

"What makes you think there are armed men in my house?"

"The ghost was there! He saw them!"

"The ghost? That pesky ghost actually did go to my house?"

"Yes! And there are two dangerous men inside right now!"

"I'm sorry, Sam, but I just don't believe that ghost is telling the truth. He doesn't like me, and he no doubt thinks this little prank is funny."

Samantha covered the receiver and turned to Jason. "Are you lying to me?" she asked sharply. "Because if you are. . . "

"I'm not lying, Sam. They're making their way toward the front of the house right now. They heard Bruce's car pull up, and they're checking it out."

"Bruce! This is no joke. Those men are looking at you through the window right now."

"I don't see anyone at a window."

"More trouble, Sam!" Jason barked. "They've seen Bruce on the mobile phone. They think he is calling the police."

"Bruce, get out of there fast! They think you're calling the police!"

Suddenly a shot rang out from inside the house. Glass shattered from the window just behind Bruce's head. Even before the last piece of flying glass hit the floor the Lexus was moving backward, tires screeching, and black smoke from burning rubber pouring into the air.

The burglars fired a second shot, striking the car in the trunk as it sped away into the night.

"What's happened?!" Samantha screamed into the phone.

"He's a little busy right now, Sam. He can't answer you," Jason replied.

"Is he all right?"

"He's safe for now, but the two men are about to leave the scene in a van loaded with stolen goods from his house. The license number of the van is ATR 696."

After a long delay, Bruce spoke over the phone again. "Samantha, darling, the ghost wasn't lying! Someone shot at me!"

"Where are you now, Bruce?"

"I'm a few blocks from my house."

"The robbers are moving east on 40th Street," Jason reported. "Hang up the phone, Sam, and call the police. Maybe we can help catch these guys."

"Bruce, the robbers are driving east on 40th Street. They're in a white van, license number ATR 696."

"They must be right behind me! I'm headed east on 40th Street too! They're trying to kill me! What shall I do?"

Samantha's face was stone white. "Go to him," she said to Jason. "See if there's anything you can do to help."

"What can I do, Sam? I'm virtually helpless."

"Just try!"

Jason watched as Bruce glanced in his rear mirror. "They're right behind me!" he screamed. "I'm going to be killed!"

Sure enough, the white van was closing the gap behind them. Jason yelled into the phone, "tell Bruce to turn right at the next corner!" Samantha fired Jason's instructions back to Bruce.

At the next intersection, Bruce darted right at high speed. In his haste, he misjudged the turn and struck the curb. The Lexus was thrown from the pavement and shot through mid-air into the left hand lane of the cross street. For half a block, the car swerved violently between lanes as the frightened man fought to bring it under control.

"What are you doing, trying to kill me again?" Jason shouted. The van sped on through the intersection, still moving east at high speed.

Bruce pulled into the parking lot of a Circle K and parked the car. He sat shaking violently. For a time, he was unable to answer Samantha, who was frantically calling his name on the car phone. At last he spoke. "I've lost them, Samantha. At least for the moment."

"Are you all right, Bruce? Are you hurt?"

"I think I'm all right."

"Tell him to call the police!" Jason yelled into the phone. "I'm going to check on those guys in the van."

Several minutes passed before Jason returned to find Samantha nervously pacing the floor in the kitchen. "I know where the robbers are headed," he said. "What's going on at this end?"

"Two police officers are with Bruce now, taking a report on the crime."

"Can you get him back on the car phone?"

"I think so."

The phone rang only once before Bruce answered. "Hello, darling, is that you?"

"Yes, it's me. Are the officers still with you?"

"It's my fiancee."

"What did you say, Bruce?"

"Oh, sorry, darling. I was speaking to Officers Brady and Samson. They wanted to know who I was talking to on the phone."

"Quick, Sam!" Jason interrupted, "tell him the robbers are heading for a place called Silvester's Packing House."

"Bruce, the ghost knows where the robbers are now. They're on their way to a place called Silvester's Packing House."

"Hold on, darling. Do either of you officers know of a place called Silvester's Packing House?"

"Yes, sir," Officer Brady answered. "I know the place. It's on Waterfront Drive."

"Well," Bruce said in a shaky voice, "I've just learned the robbers are on their way there, right now. They're in a white van, license number ATR 696."

"Now how could you possibly know that, Mr. Vincent?"

"How do I know? It's a long story, but believe me I do know it. If you send someone there immediately, you can catch these men red-handed."

After a long pause, Officer Brady turned to his partner. "Murphy, call it in. Let's see if this fellow knows what he's talking about."

"Thanks, officer." Bruce sighed.

"You'd better hold your thanks until we see if those guys are where you say they are. If this is a hoax. . . "

"It's no hoax, officer. My girlfriend is a psychic."

"Good thinking!" Samantha laughed. "That should come close to satisfying them, at least."

"A psychic, eh?" Officer Brady said, tilting his hat back on his head. "I don't put much stock in such things, but we'll see." He turned and walked slowly back to his patrol car.

"You know, darling. . ." Bruce spoke with obvious difficulty. "Your ghost may have saved my life. Perhaps I have misjudged the fellow."

"Guess what?" Samantha asked Jason.

"I give up."

"Bruce thinks he may have misjudged you. He realizes you

probably saved his life."

Jason slid backward onto a kitchen chair. "Yeah, well, I may regret it yet. It would have improved my chances with you, him being a ghost, I mean."

"He says 'you're welcome,' Bruce." Samantha laughed.

"I have to hang up for now, Samantha. The officers want me at the patrol car to finish the report."

"Are you sure you're okay now?"

"Thanks to your ghost, darling, I'm fine. A little shook up, but fine, nevertheless."

Samantha hung up the phone and pulled her chair up to the table across from Jason. "I want you to know how much I appreciate what you did tonight."

"Forget it."

"It was unselfish."

"I saw the house Bruce lives in. I can see why you would consider marrying the guy."

"The thought of the house never entered my mind."

"Sam!"

"Okay, I have thought about it. It would sure beat living in this cramped apartment. But it's not like I've set the date with Bruce or anything."

"Can I take that to mean I still have a chance with you?"

"That's not fair. How can I answer a question like that, the way things are now?"

"What if Gus comes through with a solution? Will I stand a chance then?"

"All I can say is, you're still my favorite ghost. There's always a chance for anything, I suppose."

"I guess I'd better be going and let you get back to bed, huh?"

"I'd really appreciate it. And oh, could I ask you to check on Bruce one more time? Just to be sure, you know."

"I'll check on him, Sam. If anything's wrong I'll get back with you; otherwise, sleep well. I'll make sure Bruce gets tucked in."

"Thank you," she said. He smiled and slipped through the wall.

Bruce was just returning to his car after completing the last of the report. Jason took a seat on the passenger's side again. Bruce started the engine and put the car in reverse. Just then he heard his name being called.

"Hold up!" Officer Brady cried as he hurried toward the Lexus. Bruce brought the car to a stop, and the officer leaned in the open window. "That girlfriend of yours," the officer began, "what did you say her name was?"

"Do you mean my fiancee, officer?"

"That's who I mean, pal."

"Why do you want to know her name?"

"I'd like to meet that lady sometime. I don't know how she did it, but she hit it right on the head. We caught both those guys at Silvester's Packing House, just like she said."

"Well, what do you know," Jason laughed. "She really is psychic."

CHAPTER FOURTEEN

"Blockbuster Video." Samantha read the sign on the door as she pushed it open and entered the store. Browsing through the selections, she searched for just the right movie for a relaxing evening at home alone. Everyone needs some time to themselves once in awhile.

Too bad Bruce couldn't understand that a little better. It would seem that of all people, a psychologist would understand this need. She couldn't believe how upset he became when she declined his offer to see a special performance of "My Fair Lady," her favorite play. "Oh, well," she reasoned, "he'll get over it, and I desperately need to be alone."

Turning down the first aisle, she noticed a poster hanging from the ceiling advertising an adventure movie. A slogan on the poster read, "The only thing that never changes is change itself."

How true, she thought, reviewing the recent changes in her own life. The simple *pre-ghost* days were gone forever. It reminded her of passing through a one-way turnstile. She could never return to where she had been.

She considered the changes with Bruce. Was it only last month he was that comfortable, easygoing man who wanted to marry her, but was willing to give her time to think things out? Not anymore. Now he pressed constantly to have her set the date.

Her feelings for Bruce were the same as before. She knew what she felt for him was not real love. Nevertheless, being fond of him, she was sure that in time something stronger would blossom.

Then it caught her eye. *Yes,* she smiled, *this is definitely the right movie for tonight.*

"Two dollars and thirty-seven cents," the young man at the cash register said matter-of-factly. She counted out the exact change, which he rang up. Dropping the video into a plastic bag, he handed it to her over the electronic detector and turned his attention to the next customer.

The leisurely walk home invigorated Samantha and gave her time to further sort things out. *Who would have ever guessed, this time last year, that I would believe in a ghost?* she thought. She knew now that Jason had no intention of going away, and he constantly reassured her that Gus was close to a solution. The visit from her grandparents, wonderful as it was, had done little to ease her confusion.

What of her feelings toward the ghost? She wasn't exactly sure how she felt about him. It was a feeling completely different from her fondness for Bruce. She no longer resented Jason, and had to admit he was great fun to be around.

What's a girl supposed to do? she sighed. The more she pondered the problem, the further she seemed from an answer.

By this time summer had arrived, and school was over. This left her with another big decision. She usually spent the break working on her master's degree. This year, however, she just wasn't sure she could face a semester buried in the books.

Back at her apartment, she made a big bowl of popcorn and a pitcher of iced lemonade. Sliding the tape into her VCR, she settled back to enjoy a relaxed evening.

Things went as planned until near the end of the movie. She was completely engrossed in the story, and, as usual with this one, was having a good cry. Then she heard his voice.

"May I come in, Sam?"

"No!" she snapped. "Go away, I want to be alone tonight!"

"Come on, Sam, I'm lonesome. Ask me in."

"I told you to leave me alone! Now get lost!"

Tossing a few kernels of popcorn in her mouth, she turned back to the movie. A minute or so later she glanced up to see Jason standing next to her. "What are you doing?" she barked. "You know you aren't to come in here without my permission!"

"I'm lonesome, Sam. Have a heart."

"All right! You're here. Just sit down and be quiet. I want to see this movie."

"You've seen that same movie a dozen times. I know because I was there."

"Will you please shut up, and let me enjoy the ending. This is the part where he dances with her for the last time."

"What does Patrick Swayze know about being dead, anyway?"

"Don't knock Patrick. He happens to be my favorite ghost."

"Hey! I thought I was your favorite ghost!"

That was it. He had pushed her too far. Samantha dropped her popcorn and lit into him. "I deserve a break from you once in awhile! Now get out, and leave me alone!"

"Come on, Sam."

She grew even more angry. "I've had it with you! Get out of my life!"

"You want me to. . ."

Popcorn flew violently in every direction as she slammed a clenched fist against the table. "I WANT YOU TO LEAVE ME ALONE! I WANT YOU TO GO FIND SOMEONE ELSE TO HAUNT! I HOPE I NEVER SEE YOU AGAIN!"

Jason stood in silence, looking stunned. Completely ignoring him, Samantha turned her interest back to the movie. She didn't glance up again until the final scene had faded from the screen. When she did look again, Jason was nowhere to be seen.

Good, she thought. *I hope you stay gone.*

The next morning, Samantha called her best friend Arline to see if she would like to spend the day shopping. With Arline, shopping was a word that didn't have to be said twice. The two spent an enjoyable day together. They bought a few odds and ends, but mostly just window shopped while bringing each other up to date on all the latest news. Bruce took them both to dinner that evening. There was little time left during the day to think about the ghost, who was not seen.

The following Thursday morning, Samantha attended her weekly aerobics class that she had moved from Tuesday nights now that school was out. That evening, she and Bruce finally attended "My Fair Lady," keeping her mind off Jason's absence.

One week passed, then two. Samantha still heard nothing from Jason. She wondered if he had really taken her at her word. Would she ever see him again, or had her cruel tongue driven him away forever? Somehow that thought didn't seem quite as wonderful as it had a few days earlier.

Saturday morning she awoke to a melancholy day. She decided to have a Sausage McMuffin for breakfast. She spent the ride to McDonald's thinking about the ghost. At the restaurant she found herself drawn to the same booth she had shared with Jason and Bruce the night they all went on their fun date.

This is crazy, she thought. *Here I am, free of the ghost at last, and all I can do is brood about it. I should be glad to let it go.* But she couldn't.

For the first time, she began to understand something about herself. *I don't believe this,* she thought. *I miss that pesky ghost.* She started to take a bite of her sandwich, but dropped it back to the wrapper. *I miss him bad.*

Thinking it would help, she dropped by the house of one of her girlfriends. She even stayed for dinner. It didn't work. The pain of her loneliness grew even stronger.

That evening, sitting alone in her apartment, a thought came to her. *That ghost is not one to give up so easily,* she reasoned. *I'll bet he's here right now. In fact I'll bet he never really left at all.*

She walked to the living room and stared at the front door. "Okay, my ghostly friend," she said aloud, "this has gone far enough. You can come out now." There was no response.

"What do you want from me, an apology? Okay, I'm sorry. So show yourself." Still, nothing.

"That's not good enough for you? You want more?" She stared at the door. "All right, I give in. You win. I do have feelings for you. I like you." She felt pierced by the total silence. In desperation, she tried one last time.

"I like you a lot, okay?" She slipped to the sofa. "You can come back now." Her voice trailed off to a whisper. "Please, come back."

"Maybe if ya' called him by name once in awhile he'd be easier to get along with."

With a loud gasp, Samantha sprang to her feet. "Who are you?!" she demanded of the stranger in her room.

"Take it easy, Sam," he said holding out a hand in a calming gesture, "I'm Gus."

Her mouth fell open. "Oh!" she choked. "You mean, there really is a Gus?"

"In the flesh—or, so to speak, that is," he shrugged.

Samantha struggled to catch her breath as her heart slowly returned to its normal rhythm. "So you're Gus?" she asked, studying him intently. "You sure know how scare the wits out of a lady."

"Sorry, Sam."

"You don't look anything like I had pictured."

"Well, I'm sure Jason didn't paint a very perty picture of me. He's kind of angry, ya' know—about the typo, I mean."

"Are you telling me there really is a contract, like he said, and you did make the typo on it?"

"Yep, it's just like he told ya'. I messed things up good, don'cha think?"

"I guess so."

"You hurt him too, ya' know. Just because he's a ghost doesn't mean he has no feelins."

"You called him a ghost—is that really what he is? He denies it, you know."

"I know, but take it from me, he's a ghost all right. Ya' don't have to tell him I said that, though. He's mad enough at me already."

"Would you like to sit down?"

"No thanks, Sam. I'll just stand if ya' don't mind."

"Do you mind if I sit?"

"Of course not, Sam. It's your house."

"How did I hurt him?" she asked, sliding to the sofa.

"Well, the worst way is by not usin' his name."

"Is he really . . . ?"

"In love with ya'?"

"Yes, Gus. Is he really in love with me?"

"Did Romeo love Cleopatra?"

"That's Juliet, Gus. Romeo loved Juliet."

"You know what I mean. I always did get those folks mixed up, that didn't have a contract. Anyway, yes, he loves ya'. He loves ya' a lot."

"All right, let's get down to some facts. Everyone wants me to spend the rest of my life with him. Now I ask you, what kind of life would we have together? There is a big social difference, you know."

"I know, Sam. Believe me, I'm workin' on it."

"You do realize, I'm probably going to marry Bruce."

"Bad mistake."

"You can't stop me—can you?"

"No, Sam, I can't stop ya', but it's a bad mistake, anyway." Gus walked to the mantel where he picked up a picture of Bruce. "Just what is it ya' see in this guy anyway?" he asked.

"You picked up that picture!" she exclaimed in surprise.

"Yeah, well, ya' see, I'm not exactly bound by the same restrictions as Jason."

"You can do things he can't do?"

"You got it. Anyhow, Sam, what do ya' find so great about this Bruce fella?"

"Bruce is a very kind, considerate, thoughtful man."

"Do ya' love him?"

"Well, I'm—fond of him."

Returning to where she was seated, he reached for her left hand. "That's some rock you got in that ring, Sam."

"I like it," she answered, a little surprised at being able to feel his touch. "I can feel your hand, Gus!"

"I told ya', Sam, I'm not a ghost. I passed that stage centuries ago."

"You were a ghost at one time?"

"Everybody has to go through that stage, but don't ask me more about that. I'm limited on what I can tell ya' about it."

"Will I ever be able to feel . . . you know?"

"His name is Jason."

"Will I ever feel his touch on my hand?"

"Not as long as things are the way they are now, ya' won't."

"And you're trying to find a way to change that, right?"

"Actually, Sam, I already have it figured out."

"You've what?"

"I have the answer, right now."

"Well then, do you mind telling me what you're waiting for?"

"It's you, Sam, yer not ready yet. I got to be sure yer in love with Jason, before I can go any further. When the time's right, I'll make my move, but not before."

"I don't understand."

"You will, Sam. In time. Anyhow, ya' never did answer my

question about Bruce. Is it his money?"

Samantha blushed. "I admit," she said shyly, "it would be nice. Not living in a place like this. Not forever, I mean."

"Well, at least yer honest about it."

"I don't mean to make it sound like I have no feelings for Bruce. Actually, I'm very fond of him. He is a good man, and I honestly think I could be happy with him."

"How do ya' feel about Jason?"

This question caught Samantha by surprise. She needed some time to think before answering. "I'm not sure," she said after a bit. "I enjoy having him around."

"How would ya' feel if he never came back?"

"Oh, Gus! Don't tell me that might happen. I'd miss him immensely."

Gus took one of Samantha's hands in each of his own, and looked her right in the eye. "I want ya' to think about this, Sam. No one but you can make the choice between Bruce and Jason. Just remember that choice comes with some good, and some bad. Ya' can't have it all. If ya' choose Bruce, Jason will be gone for good. And it works the other way, too. Ya' can't have them both, so think hard on it before making the choice."

"I'll have to have some hurt either way; is that what you're saying?"

"That about sums it up," he said, dropping her hands. "Nothin' good ever comes without some pain attached to it."

She paused and looked hard at Gus, sizing up the possibility of asking him the same question she had asked her grandfather. Gathering all her courage, she went for it.

"I have a question, Gus, and my grandad said you're the one who can answer it."

"Ya' want to know if Bruce is covered by a special contract?"

"How did you know that?"

"Yer grandaddy already brought it up. He talked ta me about it when he turned in his temporary pass."

"Well, does he have a contract?"

"Nope."

"So, just for the sake of argument, let's say everything worked out like you want, with Jason and me. What happens to Bruce?"

"He'll get over it."

"No! I won't do it. It's one thing for me to bring pain on myself, but I can't bear the thought of bringing pain to him. If you ever expect me to choose Jason, then you can just find someone else who would make Bruce happy."

"Sam, I just handle the contracts, I don't choose who gets them."

"I didn't say you had to have a contract for Bruce, just find someone for him and set up the match. Grandad tells me you're quite a horse trader; I'm sure a thing like that is within your ability. And don't forget, I'm fully aware of the trouble you're in with the higher authorities over this thing."

"Ya' drive a hard bargain, Sam. I'll give it some thought. But for now, let's get you and old Jason together."

"When can I see him again, Gus?"

"Well, I don't know. Ya' did hurt him perty bad."

"How can I make it up to him?"

"Let him know ya' want him back, AND use his name once in a while."

"Will you give him the message for me?"

"Give it to him yerself . . . he's right outside yer front door."

"He's what?!"

"You heard me," Gus answered, with a silly grin filling his face.

Samantha sprang from the sofa and dashed to the door. Throwing it open she rushed into the hall, where to her great delight, she found Gus was right. Jason was there. Her heart felt like it was doing cartwheels as their eyes met. In a whisper she spoke. "You can come in, if you want to." He didn't move. "I mean," she added quietly, "if you want to . . . Jason."

The sound of his wild "YA-HOOO" was heard only by one person. Her ears rang for several minutes, but it was worth it.

CHAPTER FIFTEEN

Samantha heard what she thought was a knock at the door. "Is someone there?" she called, switching off the vacuum cleaner. No one answered.

Good, she thought with a sigh of relief. *I wouldn't want anyone to see me looking like this.* Her hair was a disaster, she had no makeup on, and she was wearing her old, comfortable, timeworn yellow robe. The one she always wore when she cleaned her apartment.

Just as she was about to switch the Hoover back on, the knock came again. This time there was no mistaking it.

"Who is it?" she called a second time, desperately trying to brush back her hair with one hand.

Again, there was no answer. *That's strange,* she thought, moving cautiously to the door. Without releasing the safety chain, she slid it open an inch or so and peered through the crack into the hall. It seemed to be unoccupied. Then she noticed them.

Quickly disconnecting the safety chain, she threw open the door. She had never seen a more beautiful arrangement of red roses.

What a nice surprise, Bruce, she beamed, searching the hall both ways. She puzzled how the one delivering them could vanish so swiftly, but soon dismissed the thought.

After placing the flowers in the center of the coffee table next to the sofa, she counted them one by one. "A dozen," she said cheerfully. "Bruce, you're in good with me this time."

The card lay in the fold of a large gold ribbon surrounding the vase. Carefully removing the envelope, she opened it and read the note.

I don't believe it! she gasped, noticing how the note was signed. *How could he have . . . ?* Bruce hadn't sent the flowers at all. She sank slowly to the sofa and read the message.

Sam,

These roses are a token of my feelings for the most beautiful schoolteacher I have ever known. I'm sure Bruce got the credit at first, but I don't mind. I only hope your surprise was a pleasant one. You see, Sam, I am courting you. True, I have a big handicap, but I am courting you. Bruce takes you on dates all the time, and I wanted my chance. I asked the help of some close friends. You may think this is crazy, but please, Sam, I beg you, give it a chance. Go out with me tonight. If you accept, and you had better or you'll break my heart, wear your finest evening gown. Be ready at eight-thirty sharp. Now, beautiful lady, just give your answer, yes or no. I'll get the message.

With love, your favorite ghost.

Clutching the letter to her heart, she sprang from the couch. "Yes!" she cried, dancing in a circle like a music box ballerina. "Yes, you crazy ghost, I accept. Pick me up at eight-thirty, and don't be late!"

She took much longer than usual getting ready. Everything had to be just right. Not one hair out of place, not one wrinkle in her gown.

Then came the wait. Unquestionably, it took at least two hours for the hands on her clock to move from the eight to the eight-thirty mark. At last, the big hand moved its final fraction of an inch. She sat perfectly still, staring at the door, listening intently over the sound of her own heartbeat. Then it came. It was his voice. "Sam, it's me. May I come in?"

"Not until I open the door," she exclaimed. "Tonight, you walk through it in the normal way."

Opening the door, she gasped with excitement at the sight of him. He wore his full dress army uniform, including a large medal pinned neatly to the left side of his chest. "My, aren't you the handsome one!" she said. "You may come in, sir."

Jason didn't move, but stood frozen for a long time, just looking at her. She wore a black velvet fitted evening gown, with pearl earrings and a matching necklace. "Wow!" he said at last. "You've never looked more beautiful, Sam."

"Thank you," she answered, "and I must say, you look pretty sharp yourself—for a ghost, I mean."

He broke out laughing. "You just had to do that, didn't you?"

"Would you want me to be any other way?"

"I suppose not, Sam. But you know what the best part is?"

"No, Jason, what is the best part?"

"You dressed like that for me. Not for old what's-his-name."

"Are you planning to stand in the hall all night, or would you like to come in?" He stepped inside, and she closed the door.

"I have no idea how you plan on dating me. I thought you couldn't do things like this."

"I had a lot of help, and I have a great evening planned. You're going to love it, pretty lady."

"I'm at your mercy, kind sir. It's up to you to find a way to get us where we're going—wherever that is."

"Sorry, darling," he said trying to sound as much like Bruce as possible. "My Lexus is in the garage having the air in the tires changed, so we will just have to do without it tonight."

"No Lexus?" she teased. "I think maybe I'll just cancel the whole thing, then."

"It's okay, Sam. I've found a way to get there without the Lexus. This way please, my lady," he said, extending a bent elbow in her direction. She slipped her arm through his in pretend fashion, and followed him in the direction of the living room wall.

"Am I going to walk through a wall too?" she asked, a little reluctantly.

"Trust me."

"Okay," she said, trying to hide her anxiety, "but I hope you know what you're doing."

Just as she was about to step into the wall, a strange and exciting thing happened. The wall seemed to part, like a pair of floor-length drapes opening at the pull of the cord. The two stepped effortlessly through the opening. Samantha drew a deep breath as she found herself in the most stunningly elegant ballroom she had ever seen. In the center of the large room, surrounded by marble pillars, was one table, set for two to dine. Three unlighted candles in a silver candelabra decorated the center of the table. The soft light of the room danced in dazzling color, reflected from a thousand crystals on the overhead chandelier. A delightful aroma filled the room, and for some reason it seemed strangely familiar. Soft music added charm to the evening, though no orchestra could be seen.

"I'm impressed, Jason. This is fabulous."

"Better than any place old Bruce ever took you?"

"Bruce who?"

"Oh, yeah!" Jason shouted, savoring his moment of triumph. With a cheerful bounce in his step, he escorted Samantha to the table where they seated themselves across from each other.

From somewhere behind Samantha a waiter hurriedly appeared, whispered something to Jason, then walked quickly away.

"That waiter," she smiled, "looked amazingly like your probation officer."

"Hey, good help is hard to find, especially for a guy in my position."

"He's perfect, Jason. By the way, what did he say to you, or is it a secret?"

"Sorry, Sam. It seems I missed one of my cues. I made a big mistake."

"What kind of mistake?"

He pointed to the empty glass on the table in front of her. "Pick it up, Sam."

"Pick up my glass?"

"Please."

When she reached for the glass, she was shocked to discover that her hand passed through it, like it wasn't there. "I don't understand," she said.

"We have to change places."

"Change places?"

"Yeah. I'm sitting on your side of the table, and you're on mine."

"Oh," she giggled, "I understand." They exchanged places.

"Sorry, Sam. I didn't plan for that to happen."

"Don't be sorry, Jason. That was kind of fun. Definitely different, but fun, nevertheless."

"Thanks, Sam," he said. "That's kind of you."

Gus, fully dressed for the part, returned to the table with two pitchers, each filled with a sparkling pink drink. "I figure ya' ta like this stuff, Sam," he said as he filled her glass from one of the pitchers. "It's like nothin ya' ever tasted before."

"Thank you, Gus."

She watched as he filled Jason's glass from the second pitcher, and listened as he explained. "Jason gets the same, only his is what ya' might call the light version."

Samantha took a sip from her glass. "This is delicious!"

"Would you say, sort of heavenly?" Jason chuckled.

Returning her glass to the table, she stared at him. "You know what you are, Jason? You're a nut."

"Ya' got that right," Gus agreed as he walked away.

"You're a fun nut to be with though," she added, gazing dreamily at his face and thinking how handsome he looked. *Much more fun,* she thought to herself, *than Bruce.*

Her attention turned to the medal he wore, which she recognized as the Distinguished Service Cross. *Have I underestimated him?* she wondered. *Maybe he was a John Wayne-type hero.*

Just then Gus returned pushing a cart. Samantha struggled to keep from laughing. He was trying so hard to be the perfect waiter. Again, there were two of everything on the tray.

First he served them each a fresh garden salad, rich in thick blue cheese dressing. Next, he lifted the lid from a large two-part silver chafing dish.

"Chicken and dumplings?" she asked in surprise.

Gus froze where he stood. "Is there somethin' wrong with chicken 'n dumplins, Sam?"

"No, of course not. I love the dish, but it seems out of place in these surroundings."

"Ya' got a point there," he said, spooning a hearty helping on her plate from one side of the silver chafing dish. "I think, though, you'll understand when ya' taste it." Gus filled Jason's plate from the other half of the silver chafing dish.

Lifting a linen napkin from a small straw basket, Gus removed one of two steaming hot miniature loaves of freshly baked bread. He carefully placed the first one on Samantha's plate. It smelled wonderful.

"Oh, Gus!" she squealed in delight. "May I?"

"By all means," he agreed.

Pinching off a piece of the bread, she blew on it to cool it a bit, then slipped it into her mouth. "I knew it!" she shouted. "It's Grandma's sourdough bread!"

"That's right," Jason beamed, as Gus placed the second loaf on his plate.

"And the chicken and dumplings?"

"They are your grandmother's, too."

"Oh, Jason, what a wonderful surprise! I wish I could kiss you!"

Jason drew a deep breath. "I wish you could kiss me too, Sam. It feels pretty good, though, just knowing you'd like to."

Suddenly, each of the three candles on the table flickered into a soft blue flame. Samantha glanced at Gus, who shrugged. "Sorry, Sam. I forgot the matches."

"I forgive you, Gus. You did great. I've never seen anything more romantic in my life."

Jason's feelings were obvious. The look of love on his face told it all. He watched in delight as Samantha savored every bite of her grandmother's special dishes—things she had supposed she would never taste again.

"All right, Jason," she teased after finishing her second huge helping of chicken and dumplings, "where is it?"

He tried to keep a straight face, letting his eyes drift upward. "I have no idea what you're talking about, Sam."

"Don't lie to me. You know perfectly well what I'm talking about."

"Well, I suppose you could mean. . . "

"That's *exactly* what I mean. Where's my apple pie?"

"What makes you think your grandmother made an apple pie?"

"She did, and if you know what's good for you you'll quit playing games with me and get it out here—now!"

"What's that behind you, Sam?" he asked suddenly.

She whirled to look. "What are you talking about? I don't . . ." She turned back to see a plate in front of her, filled with hot apple pie.

Leaning back in his chair, he assumed a smug "I gotcha" look. "Was that fast enough to suit you?"

"Oh, ha! Aren't you the funny one. You know I want this pie bad enough that I'll let you get away with anything, don't you?"

"You got that right."

She relished the first bite while studying Jason closely. He looked so handsome in his uniform. She was seeing another side to this ghost who had been haunting her for the last few months. It was a side she had never seen before.

"Jason," she asked between bites, "did you ever date when you were—alive?"

"I dated some."

"Were you ever married?"

"I wanted to marry. I spent my lifetime looking for the right one."

"And you never found her?"

"Oh, I found her." There was a definite quiver in his voice. "The only trouble is by the time I found her, I was in no condition to marry, and she was only five years old." He reached across the table and in a make-believe manner, stroked her hand. "I've been courting her ever since," he added.

She looked tenderly into his moist eyes, but didn't answer. In her mind, however, she did admit that his courting had improved immensely.

The music ended and a new song began to play. It was an instrumental version of "The Tennessee Waltz."

"That's one of my favorite songs from my youth," Jason said. "Will you dance with me, Sam?"

"Can we do that?" she asked.

"If we pretend a lot, we can."

The two moved slowly around the room to the rhythm of the waltz. "This is fun," she admitted, and jokingly observed how light he was on his feet.

He laughed. "Take my word for it, Sam. That's only because you can't feel my feet."

They danced until the last note of the waltz faded away, then walked slowly back to the table. "Will you do me a favor, Jason?

Make sure you seat me on my own side this time."

The table had been cleared while they were on the dance floor. Now, nothing separated them but a vase holding a single rose.

"That rose," she said, looking mystified. "It's fluorescent blue. I've never seen anything like it. Are all flowers that radiant over here?"

"Don't ask me, okay? That's just one more thing I don't understand yet. There is something I do understand, though," he said softly. "There's no way I can give you a ring, like Bruce did."

"Jason. . . "

"No, Sam. Let me finish. I wanted to say, I do have another gift for you."

"A gift?"

"I hope you'll like it. Look on the floor, next to your chair."

She looked, and there she found a small black jewelry box, which she picked up and laid on the table in front of her.

"Go ahead, Sam. Open it up."

Carefully she lifted the lid and glanced inside to see a medal. It looked almost identical to the one on Jason's coat, except the ribbon was missing and it was attached to a lovely gold chain. "It's beautiful," she said, lifting it from the box.

"Do you really like it?" he asked.

"I love it, but I don't understand. How can you give this to me?"

"It's mine," he explained. "What you see on my chest is what you might call its ghost. The medal and gold chain in your hand have been gathering dust in my brother's attic for the last twenty years. The chain was my mother's. I wanted to give you something, so I asked for Gus's help. He found these things where I said they would be and had them made into a necklace."

"How did he do that?"

"Gus can do anything. He has friends everywhere."

"He is a rather amazing guy."

"Oh, Sam. I love you so much. I know if you'll give it time, that amazing guy can fix my problem, too."

Samantha slid the chain around her slender neck and closed the fastener. "It's beautiful, Jason, and so is the thought behind it. By the way," she asked, "how did you win the medal?"

"He won't tell ya', Sam, but I will." It was Gus. "There was a fire in the barracks. Even the professional firefighters gave up on the five men trapped inside. Not Jason, though. He got 'em all out. He wore the scars from the fire the rest of his life. He wasn't so handsome ta look at back then. The scars were removed when he got his new face, after choking on the chicken bone."

"Wow, Jason. The more I learn about you, the more amazed I am. You were quite a man. After tonight, I have to admit—you still are."

Turning to Gus, she asked, "Does that hidden orchestra of yours play requests?"

"Name it, kid."

"One of my favorites is called 'Now and Forever.' It was done by Air Supply."

"I can fix ya' up with the song. Air Supply, I can't manage. They're still on yer side, ya' know."

"I'll take it, maestro."

Reaching his hand high into the air, he snapped his fingers. Instantly the music stopped and her request was granted.

"Thank you, Gus." Before he could react, she had jumped to her feet and kissed him on the cheek. His face turned brilliant red.

From that moment on, for the rest of the night, the two danced. At least it was close enough to dancing, and they both enjoyed it immensely. Cradled in the joy of each other's company, they lost all track of time until Gus returned.

"Sorry, kids," he said reluctantly, "the clock is about to strike midnight, and ya' both know what that means, don't ya'?"

"It probably means the ball is over," she sighed.

"Yep, I could only get the hall till midnight. I managed that because the head janitor owed me a favor. I'm sorry to say, Sam, no glass slipper goes with this story."

"Do I get to keep the necklace?"

"That ya' do," Gus beamed.

"Then what more can I ask? I'd only wind up breaking a glass slipper, anyway."

Jason offered her his arm again. Retracing the path that had brought them to the world "between," they were once again back in her apartment.

"I hope you enjoyed it, Sam."

"Oh, Jason," she answered with glistening eyes, "it was the best date this schoolteacher has ever been on."

It was very late into the night before the thrill of the evening subsided and allowed Samantha's mind to finally drift into sleep.

Chapter Sixteen

"Hello?" Samantha said, answering her phone.

"Hi, Sam. It's me, Arline. Want to take in a movie and do some shopping?"

"What's playing?"

"I don't know, who cares? I need an excuse to get out of doing my housework. And I've been looking at this great pants set. I want your opinion."

"You've convinced me. Let's do it."

"Great! Meet me at the mall in an hour, in front of the theater."

Samantha hung up the phone, changed clothes, and hurried to the bus stop.

The movie was a "full tissue box" tearjerker, Arline's favorite kind. The two women sat engrossed in the story, eating buttered popcorn and drinking diet soda. Suddenly, during one of the saddest scenes, Samantha broke into spontaneous laughter.

"What's the matter," Arline fussed, "are you losing it? This is not a comedy."

"I'm sorry," Samantha managed, trying to compose herself. "I just thought of something funny that happened to me last week." *How can I tell her there's a ghost in the seat next to me, telling dumb jokes?* Samantha thought.

"Well, try to control yourself. I can't enjoy a movie like this without a good cry, and I can't have a good cry with you laughing." Arline took a handful of popcorn and turned her attention back to the big screen.

Samantha choked back her laughter. Without allowing Arline to see what she was doing, she waved a hand at Jason, trying to shut him up.

Jason grinned, obviously enjoying his little game. "By the way, pretty schoolteacher, did I ever tell you about the poem I wrote when I was still alive?"

Jason, you nut! Stop embarrassing me like this.

"It was about a fly."

I'm not listening to you! I am not listening to you!

"Once there lived a tiny fly. . . "

I will not laugh at your jokes! She took a drink of soda.

"A fly who had but just one eye."

"Excuse me," she said, getting up from her seat and handing the bucket of popcorn to Arline. "I have to powder my nose."

"Right now? I think he's going to kiss her; can't you wait?"

"One day he fell from rather high, and right away began to cry."

"No, I can't wait!" she cried, pushing past Arline to the aisle. She rushed to the door, threw it open, and darted to the hall. Once outside, she burst into laughter. Jason was right behind her.

"Oh how sad that tiny fly, for he discovered by and by. . ."

"Jason, stop it!" she whispered sharply, when she was sure no one else was in the hall. "This is not the least bit funny!"

"That due to having just one eye. . . "

"I'm not listening to you!"

"He could but cry a half a cry."

She broke out laughing again. "That's sick. You didn't really write that, did you?"

"I most certainly did," he bragged. "Want to hear the one I wrote about the elephant?"

"Gag me!"

"Ooooh, that smarts, Sam. I'm sensitive about my poetry."

"What am I going to do with you? Go away and let me enjoy a day with my best friend."

"Oh please, fair maiden," he cried, falling to one knee, "cast me not out from thy presence, for thou knowest I love thee. Grant unto me the pleasure of thy company."

"All right, you can stay, but only if you behave yourself. Stop embarrassing me in front of Arline."

"Thy wish is my command, beautiful damsel. Take again thy seat at the theater, and I shall remain quiet as a volcano."

"Jason!"

"A mouse, I shall remain quiet as a mouse."

"You'd better!" she said, returning to the theater.

"Would you mind moving over, Arline, so I can sit next to the aisle? You know, in case I have to leave again." Arline moved without taking her eyes from the movie screen.

"That was uncalled for," Jason said smugly. "You know I wanted to sit next to you." She only smiled.

Things settled down for half an hour or so, until a scene in the movie found the hero being dragged from the girl's room by two uniformed officers. She threw herself across the bed, crying uncontrollably. Suddenly Jason appeared on the screen next to her. "I'm sorry, Scarlet," he cried loudly. "I warned you from the beginning not to get hooked on me. I love only Sam, and none other. I can recommend a good psychologist, though, if you need one."

Samantha bit her lip and sank deep into the seat, fighting to remain silent, even though inside she was exploding with laughter. Arline glanced over and noticed the tears in her eyes that couldn't be held back.

"I knew it," she said, poking Samantha's shoulder. "You're crying, too. Don't you ever laugh at me again for crying in a movie."

After the show the two women headed straight for Casual Corners. "How do you like it?" Arline asked, holding up a dark green pantsuit.

"I don't know until I see it on you." Arline disappeared into the dressing room. A few minutes later she came out wearing the outfit and a big smile.

"What do you think?"

"I love it," Samantha answered. "It's really. . ." Then she saw him. He was in the arms of a scantily-clad female mannequin, pretending to kiss it. She lost it right there. She hadn't laughed that hard since the ninth-grade cafeteria food fight.

"Well!" Arline snapped. "I guess that pretty well sums up how you feel about it."

"No, please," Samantha begged. "I really love it; it looks fantastic on you. I can't help it, I just have a case of the giggles today."

Arline stared at her cautiously. "Are you sure it looks okay?"

"I told you, it's great. You deserve it; buy it!"

"All right, I will," she said, returning to the dressing room, all smiles.

"Jason Hackett!" Samantha scolded as he walked over to her. "I've had it with you!" Searching through her purse, she found a tissue and wiped her eyes. "Please go away, and let me enjoy some time with Arline."

"Okay," he agreed. "If I can come by tonight and watch TV with you."

"It's a deal, if you promise not to recite any more poems."

"You really know how to hurt a guy, Sam."

"Get out of here, you big nut, or I swear I'll tell Arline about you."

"Go ahead. She looks pretty sharp in that pantsuit. Maybe I'll drop you and haunt her for a while."

"Are you trying to make me jealous?"

"Would you be jealous if I did like her?"

"That's for me to know, and you to wonder about. Now get out of here before she comes out again."

Jason gave her a pretend kiss on the cheek, and left. A few minutes later Arline came out of the dressing room carrying the green pantsuit.

The sales clerk dropped the receipt in the sack with the new outfit and handed it to Arline. "Thank you," she said with a smile, "and do shop at Casual Corners again."

"I will, every chance I get, you can bet on it."

"How about a frozen yogurt?" Arline asked as the two left Casual Corners. "I'll treat."

"Make it chocolate, and you've got a deal."

"What other kind is there?" she chuckled. They made their way through the mall toward the food court.

After passing four stores, and only pausing to look in the window of three, Arline spoke again. "You're acting peculiar today, Sam. Why not open up and tell doctor 'best friend' what's going on."

"You always could see right through me. I do have a problem, and it's one I could use some advice with."

"So, let's have it."

Samantha put on a big grin. "I'm being haunted by a ghost."

Arline's laugh was loud enough to attract the attention of everyone around. "Now, that's not your everyday problem. Is his name Casper, by any chance?"

"No. His name is Jason, and he's in love with me."

Arline raised an eyebrow. "Have you been eating too much Red Baron pizza lately?"

"No way! My ghost is real. He's no actor in a commercial."

"I think you've been sniffing your fingernail polish again, Sam." Arline thought a moment, then asked, "Is he cute? Your ghost, I mean."

"He's very handsome, and he's a real gentleman."

"Okay, Sam, I'll play your game. How about you? Are you in love with him?"

The smile faded from Samantha's face. She didn't answer right away. "I'm not sure," she said at length.

Arline studied her carefully, but made no immediate reply. They reached the frozen yogurt counter, where she ordered two large chocolate cones. Only after they had taken a seat at a nearby table did she speak again.

"Does Bruce know about this ghost?"

Samantha took a deep breath. "Yes," she answered. "Bruce knows about him."

"Well, what does he think about it all?"

"Bruce dislikes him immensely."

"Samantha," Arline said, looking her in the eye, "Jason is no ghost, is he? There's another man in your life, isn't there?"

"I told you he was a ghost. Are you doubting my word?"

"Are you involved with a married man?"

"Now why would you think a thing like that, Arline?"

"I know you're trying to tell me something with this ghost story; I'm just not sure what it is. You are still planning to marry Bruce, aren't you?"

"I don't know. I'm a little confused about things right now. But enough about me. Eat your yogurt."

Arline refused to drop the subject. "Look, I've never been able to understand what it is you see in Bruce, but you are wearing his ring. That should mean you owe him something, shouldn't it?"

"I'm sure I'll end up married to Bruce. It's just that I have other things to think about right now."

"By other things, you mean the ghost?"

"Yes!" she said, a tear forming in the corner of her eye. "The ghost."

"Are you going to tell me the truth? What exactly is it you're calling a ghost?"

"He's a ghost. You can believe me, or not believe me as you choose. If you don't like the idea of him being a ghost, then make up something else. He is real, he does love me, and he has me very confused."

"I don't know why you won't tell me the whole story, but what kind of a best friend would I be if I didn't trust you? We'll call him a ghost, okay? Now, do you want to talk about him?"

"Yes, Arline," she answered, the tears now flowing freely. "I would like to talk about him. He's the best thing that ever happened to me. I have so much fun just being around him."

"I'll ask you again. Do you love him?"

"I'm not sure. I feel completely different about him than I feel about Bruce, that's all I can say."

"Why not just give Bruce his ring back, and stick with this—ghost?"

"It's not that simple, Arline. Unless a miracle should happen, the ghost and I could never have a normal life together."

Arline handed Samantha a napkin, as her untouched yogurt was beginning to melt. "If you didn't want that thing, why didn't you say so before I wasted a dollar?"

"I'm sorry," Samantha said, wiping up the spill and taking a big bite. "Maybe we should change the subject. I know how hard it is for you to part with your money."

"I really wish you would tell me the whole thing," Arline said, shaking her head slowly. "Just remember, though, I'm always here if you need to talk. You know I won't think less of you, no matter what."

"I know, Arline, and thanks. Just talking to you this much has helped a bunch. Now hurry up and get that yogurt down. We still have to find something for me to buy."

CHAPTER SEVENTEEN

The August calendar was rapidly running out of days, and soon another school year would begin. After talking to Arline, Samantha had finally admitted to herself what she had refused to recognize for so long. She was falling in love—with a ghost.

Thinking often of the roller coaster adventure she had shared with Bruce and Jason, she contemplated how her life had become like that ride. One minute she crested the hill of fantasy, the next she sank to the depths of reality. In fantasy, her life was filled with the excitement of this wonderful ghost who was stealing her heart away. In reality, it was an impossible relationship, filled with discouragement and despair.

Expressing her love for Jason was impossible. True, they could see one another, they could talk and enjoy each other's company, but they could not touch. How empty it all seemed without being able to touch.

Perhaps Bruce was right, after all. Maybe she should wake up to reality, marry him, and get on with her life. Good old dependable Bruce. At least when he kissed her, she could feel it. She struggled with the thought that Bruce might never be a man who could make her happy. It would be much easier if he only knew how to have fun. Could she ever change him? She needed to find out for herself. Picking up the phone, she dialed his home number.

"Hello?"

"Hi, Bruce. Am I interrupting anything important?"

"Of course not, darling. I always have time to talk to you. What's up?"

"I was wondering, do you have anything planned for tonight?"

"I was going to call later, and ask you to attend a party at my neighbor's house. He didn't send me an invitation, but I talked him into letting us come anyway."

"I don't want to attend the party, Bruce. I want to do something fun with you for a change."

"I hope, my dear, your plans don't include any more roller coaster rides."

She laughed. "No, I won't ask you to do that again. I'd like to do something we both enjoy. You told me once you had a friend in the motion picture business who owned a private beach."

"Yes, that would be Howard Placard."

"I want to walk barefoot on the beach with you, Bruce. Do you think you can arrange with Howard to use his beach?"

"I'm certain I can. When would you like go?"

"I want to go tonight."

"Tonight? That's rather short notice, isn't it?"

"If you want to make me happy, you'll phone Howard as soon as I hang up. I want to walk barefoot on the beach with you tonight."

"Very well, darling," he conceded. "I'll do my best."

"And one more thing," she said, pressing her luck. "I don't want to go in your Lexus this time."

"What do you mean, Samantha? It's the only car I own."

"I want you to rent a red sports car. Make it a convertible."

"Samantha!"

"You heard me, Bruce. I want to teach you how to have fun. If you still want to marry me, then you had better start taking lessons, and this is the first one."

Two hours later Bruce picked Samantha up, in front of her apartment building, in a red Mustang convertible. By the time they reached Howard's private beach, he had learned to at least tolerate it.

"This is lovely, Bruce," Samantha sighed as they walked hand-in-hand along the water's edge on a deserted section of the beach. "I love the smell of salt air and the feel of warm sand between my toes." She had removed her shoes and was carrying them in her free hand. Bruce kept his on.

"I'm glad you're enjoying it, darling," he said lackadaisically.

The sun was just beginning to set on the horizon over the water, creating a spectacular view. The sound of a gentle surf, combined with a cool breeze against her face, filled Samantha with sensuous pleasure.

"Perhaps this is a good idea, darling," Bruce said as they walked. "This is a perfect place to talk of our future."

"Let's not ruin this, Bruce. Please don't pressure me for a marriage date tonight."

"Samantha," he pleaded, "we have to talk about it. We can't keep putting it off forever. And you must understand how I feel about this ghost fellow. I can't stand the thought of him being around you. For all I know, he's here with us right now."

"He's not here, Bruce. He gave me his word to leave us alone tonight. Now relax, and enjoy yourself."

"How do you know you can trust him?"

"When he gives his word on something, he keeps it."

"You once told me he gave you his word to leave us alone once we're married. Is that right?"

"Yes, he gave his word on that." Samantha turned her head so Bruce wouldn't notice the tear she had to wipe away. "And I'm sure he meant it," she added as soon as she could speak again.

Bruce stepped in front of her. "Don't you see, darling? That alone is reason enough for us to marry now. Please give me your answer tonight."

Moving to one side, she slipped around him and continued walking. He caught up in two steps. She sighed in disappointment, having hoped he would be a little more fun in these surroundings. Maybe she just needed to try harder. "You see that big rock up ahead?" she asked excitedly. "I'll bet I can beat you to it."

She gave him a hard shove, knocking him to the ground, then took off running full speed in the direction of the rock.

By the time Bruce reached the rock, Samantha was sitting on it waiting for him. She was glad to see he was at least smiling. "Samantha, darling," he said, "I never know what to expect from you. I wish I could learn to love life the way you do. I must admit, I just don't know how." He slid his arms around her and kissed her lips.

"Take off your shoes," she said.

"Darling, please."

"Bruce!"

He removed his shoes, and the two resumed their walk along the beach as the last glimpse of the sun dipped below the horizon. "I want to go to your parents' house," Samantha said after a bit. "I need a place where I can think things out. The mountain setting behind their home is the best place I know of for that. Will you take me there, Bruce?"

"Certainly, darling. When would you like to go?"

"Tomorrow will be great."

"Tomorrow?" he choked.

"Yes! And let's take the red convertible."

CHAPTER EIGHTEEN

It was a beautiful day for a drive in the mountains. Samantha studied Bruce closely. She liked seeing his hair blowing in the breeze. "Come on, you old stuffed shirt," she said. "Admit it. You like driving this car, don't you?"

He took a deep breath. "I'm trying to like it, darling. I have to admit, though, I prefer my Lexus."

"Do your parents know we're coming, or is this going to be a surprise visit?"

Bruce glanced in her direction. "I called my mother this morning. She was thrilled to have us come. You know how much she likes you, Samantha."

"I like her, too, Bruce. She's a wonderful friend to me."

"I've been meaning to ask you, darling, about that necklace you're wearing. You've worn it quite a bit lately. Is it new?"

She knew the subject of the necklace would come up sooner or later; there was no way around it. Not wanting to hide the truth from Bruce, but at the same time not wanting to open a touchy subject, she chose her words carefully. "It was given to me by a friend."

"It seems to be some kind of military decoration. The friend who gave it to you wouldn't happen to be the ghost, would it?"

"What makes you think Jason gave it to me?"

"Oh, it's Jason now, is it?"

"Bruce, your fangs are showing. I think you're jealous of my ghost."

"Jealous of a ghost? That's nonsense!"

"Well, if it's nonsense, why is your eye twitching?"

Glaring at the road ahead, Bruce gripped the steering wheel with a vise-like force. "Yes!" he snapped. "I am jealous, and if you don't marry me soon, I think I'll go insane."

"Why not make an appointment with your secretary to see your-self? Some of your own counsel might do you a world of good."

"Samantha! Why is it you always have to make a joke out of everything?"

"Lighten up, Bruce. I've told you before, it goes with the territo-ry. Admit it, you wouldn't want me any other way."

He turned the Mustang off the main road and down the quarter-mile horseshoe drive to his parents' home. "Yes, darling, I do admit it. You're the best thing that's ever happened to me. Which is precise-ly why I wish to marry you—now!"

"Who knows? You may get your wish sooner than you think."

"Do you mean . . . ?"

"I mean, Bruce, I'm getting closer to an answer. Hopefully, spending this time at your parents' home will give me a chance to think things through."

"Oh, darling, you can't imagine how it makes me feel to hear you say that."

At that moment the Vincents' home came into view. Samantha looked at it longingly. Except for the pine trees, it reminded her of one she had seen in an old English movie about a wealthy Scotsman. If she could have any home she wanted, it would be one exactly like this. Mountains and all.

"Here we are, darling," Bruce said, pulling the car to a stop and killing the engine. Arm in arm, they strolled up the stone walk toward the house.

Bruce pressed the doorbell, and the sound of mellow chimes resounded clearly, echoing through the quiet mountain air. Samantha laughed at him. "I can't get over you ringing the door bell at your own parents' home."

"Do you find that strange?"

"I find that very strange."

"Actually, it's my idea. Mother thinks of it as strange, too. I don't know, it just seems to be the proper thing to do."

"Why doesn't that surprise me?" she sighed.

Bruce's mother answered the door. Ruth was a woman of remark-able poise and stunning elegance. Everything about her always looked perfect, from her shiny, silver-streaked black hair to her flawless complexion. She and Samantha had become good friends the first time they met.

"Samantha!" she exclaimed with a warm hug. "I'm so glad you came to see us."

"Thanks, Ruth. I've been wanting to come up for some time. Last night, I finally asked Bruce to bring me."

"I'm so glad you did. Have you had lunch?"

"I made your son take me to McDonald's on the way here."

"You managed to get Bruce in a McDonald's?" Ruth asked in surprise. "I can't believe it."

"He's coming around," Samantha said.

"Good for you, Bruce," Ruth said with a kiss to his cheek. "I always said Samantha's the best thing that ever happened to you."

"Yes, mother," he said answering with a kiss of his own to her cheek.

"Come, let's go in the house," Ruth said sliding her arm around Samantha. The two women stepped into the house, leaving Bruce to follow on his own.

As they entered, Bruce's father appeared from the back of the house. "Ah, Samantha," he said. "How nice that you and Bruce could come up to see us!" He reached for her hand to give it a kiss.

From the first time she met Kent, Samantha was amazed at how much Bruce resembled him. Kent was obviously older, but the resemblance was there, nevertheless. Not only did they look alike, they acted alike as well.

"Come, my dear," Ruth said, taking Samantha by the hand. "Let's take a walk in the garden. It's lovely this time of year. We can have some girl talk," she winked, "and leave these two males to their less interesting subjects."

"I'd love that," Samantha answered cheerfully. "Do you mind, Bruce?"

"No, darling, I don't mind at all. It will give me some time to talk with Father."

The garden was beautiful. It filled most of the back yard and was ablaze with color.

"It's so peaceful here," Samantha said, as the two made their way along the winding red brick walk. A gentle breeze quietly stirred some fallen leaves in their path.

"Yes, it is," Ruth agreed. "This, and the woods just beyond, are what I love most about living here."

They walked in silence a bit before Ruth spoke again. "So?" she asked. "How are things going between you and Bruce? Are the two of you getting serious?"

"Very serious, I suppose."

"Do you love him?"

Samantha hesitated, wanting to be perfectly honest without hurting Ruth's feelings. "I feel strongly for your son," she answered a moment later. "If it's not a pure love now, I'm sure in time it will grow into one."

"That's not always true," Ruth cautioned. "There are times when feelings grow the wrong way after two people are married."

"Are you trying to discourage me from marrying your son?"

"No! Of course not, my dear. You're everything and more I've always hoped for in a wife for Bruce."

"Oh," Samantha gasped. "Just look at those gorgeous yellow roses. I've never seen anything more beautiful."

Ruth smiled. Using a small pair of shears taken from her pocket, she cut a rose and handed it to Samantha.

"Thank you, Ruth. It's lovely."

"You're lovely, too, Samantha. Nothing would make me happier than having you marry Bruce. However, that must be your decision."

Samantha held the rose close, savoring its fragrance. "Ruth," she asked, "am I reading something into your words that I shouldn't, or are you warning me I might be making a mistake?"

"This is not easy for a mother," Ruth answered after a few more steps. "You see," she said thoughtfully, "Bruce is exactly like his father. When I married Kent I knew what kind of man he was, but I thought I could change him in time. That," she sighed, "proved to be a challenge that never came about."

"Are you saying you're sorry for marrying him, then?"

"Oh, no! I'm not sorry at all. It's just that I'm the one who had to make all the changes. I had to give up many things I used to enjoy. It's been worth it, I suppose. Kent loves me, and has given me a good life. Not as exciting a life as I had hoped for, but good, nevertheless."

Ruth slid her arm through Samantha's as they walked. "What I'm trying to say is, just be sure. Don't hang your hopes too high on ever changing Bruce. If you can accept him as he is, then by all means do it. The decision is yours, my dear. Make it wisely."

"I want you to know, you make my decision easier. Having you as a second mother would be wonderful."

"Why, thank you, Samantha dear."

"Hey, you two," Bruce called from the house. "What are you cooking up out there?"

"Speaking of you-know-who," Ruth grinned, with a light jab of her elbow to Samantha's side. "Looks like we're about to have company."

"Looks like," Samantha agreed.

Ruth took Samantha's hands and gave them a light squeeze. "Think about the things I've said, my dear."

"I will, and thank you, Ruth. Thank you from the bottom of my heart."

By this time Bruce had reached the two women. "Do you suppose, mother, it would be asking too much to allow me some time with this lovely lady? After all, I am the one who found her."

"I only hope, young man," she replied, "you know what a precious jewel you've found." Then, politely excusing herself, she returned to the house.

Bruce led the way to a small love seat in the center of the garden, where he sat down. "Samantha, darling, it's time we had a serious talk." He expected her to join him on the love seat. Instead, she caught a glimpse of a white swing on the opposite side of the walk.

"How delightful!" she shouted, running to the swing. "Come on, Bruce, give me a shove."

"Samantha!" he protested. "We need to talk."

"What's the matter, Bruce? Can't a psychologist push and talk at the same time?" Bruce, obviously disgusted, walked to the swing and gave her a slight push.

"Come on," she teased, "be a little more enthusiastic. Let's have some fun."

A second push sent the swing flying higher. "That's better," she laughed. "Now what is it you want to talk about?"

"This is a rather awkward way to talk."

"Sometimes, Bruce, it's better to be awkward. It keeps us humble."

With a little extra bass in his voice for emphasis, he spoke. "Samantha, love, I insist that we be married without further delay."

"I told you I'm thinking about it. Now give me another push."

"This constantly putting it off is ridiculous!" he huffed.

She grinned at him mischievously, and asked, "Are you trying to say I'm not worth the wait?"

"Of course that's not what I'm saying, Samantha!" His voice was quivering and loud. Grabbing the support chains, he yanked the swing to a stop. "I demand that you end this childish game, and for once in your life, be serious."

She planted her feet firmly on the ground, folded her arms, and did not leave the swing. "If you're not going to push me, I refuse to listen to you, Bruce."

With clenched fists held above his head, and tightened jaw, he stomped a few feet away, where he stood with his back to her. After a moment he began to relax and turned around.

"Not a bad tantrum, Bruce," she said with a faked serious look. "Actually, though, I have a couple of fifth-graders who do much better. I think a B-minus is about the best I could give for yours."

Little by little his look of anger lessened, until it turned to a smile. Then came the laughter. Soon they both were laughing.

"Oh, Samantha, my love, you are so good for me. Don't you see? I want to get this ghost thing behind us, once and for all. I want my chance to make you the happiest woman alive. Please marry me—soon."

Samantha slid from the swing and walked slowly to him. Brushing his hair back with one hand, she gently kissed his lips. "Go back to the house, Bruce. Leave me alone for awhile."

"But. . ."

"Please, Bruce."

"Yes, darling. Perhaps you're right." Returning her kiss, he turned and walked back to the house. She watched until he went inside.

A short distance into the woods, she found herself overlooking a shallow canyon alive with majestic pine trees. At the bottom of the canyon she watched the white ripples of a stream flowing swiftly along its course. The fragrance of pines and music of wind through the branches brought a wonderful feeling of pure tranquility. Looking out over this canyon gave her a feeling she was seeing something that only the word "forever" could describe.

In this peaceful setting she pondered the recent events of her life, and searched for decisions.

Thoughts of Jason flashed like a motion picture in front of her eyes. She saw again their first meeting in her apartment. How angry she had been at the time. She witnessed the walk in the park where she fed the white ducks, and felt so foolish when the boys saw her talking to thin air. The night at McDonald's, the amusement park, and Swensen's returned vividly to her mind. The most tender memory of all, however, was that of her special date with Jason, when they danced the night away.

She studied the yellow rose in her hand. How beautiful it looked, in full bloom. *Why can't this rose keep its beauty forever?* she thought. *Why must it fade and die so quickly?*

"Jason," she said, calling his name aloud, "I've never known anyone as fun to be around as you." *Why? Why couldn't they have had better teachers on the other side? If only Gus had learned to type.*

Spotting a little trail a short distance away, she followed it down to the water's edge. There, in a shallow pool near the edge of the stream, she could see her own reflection. In her mind's eye she saw reflections of Jason and Bruce on either side of her own. Each seemed to be competing for her attention. *Only one of you can stay,* she thought, *and I must choose which it shall be.*

Just then the rose slipped from her hand, striking the surface of the water where she imagined Jason's image to be. Before she could retrieve it, it was caught in the current and swept rapidly away. Soon it rounded a bend and disappeared from sight.

She rushed to the place she had last seen the rose, but it was futile. The flower was gone forever. *How sad,* she thought, *to lose something so beautiful.* She stood for a long time, looking at the stream that had carried it away. *Now all I have left of the rose is a memory.* A warm tear rolled down her cheek. *Is that all I'll have left of you, my wonderful ghost? Will you be only a memory, too?*

Sitting on a large rock next to the bank, she watched the sunlight dance through the branches of the trees. It reminded her, again, of the day in the park with Jason.

Her thoughts shifted to Gus. Everyone who knew him had assured her he would find a way. Still, it had been over four months, and he had made no progress. She had little hope left.

More tears came as she thought of life without Jason, but she knew life held little for either of them under the circumstances.

She retraced her steps back up the trail, to where she had first stopped at the top of the canyon.

Again and again she rethought her options, but the answer was always the same. And so, standing on the edge of a mountain over-looking forever, she reached her decision.

Entering the house once again, she found Bruce and his parents at the dining room table, playing a game of Scrabble. The two men stood as she approached. "I suppose," she spoke, "Bruce has told you the real reason we came to see you today, hasn't he?"

"No," Kent responded as the three, especially Bruce, looked on in surprise.

"Well," she said, forcing a smile. "I guess I'll have to be the one to tell you. We plan to be married next week."

Scrabble pieces flew in every direction as the dictionary Bruce had been holding dropped suddenly into the middle of the game.

CHAPTER NINETEEN

"Hi, lady, it's me," came the familiar words from outside her apartment door. The sparkle in his voice pierced her heart till it ached. She knew she would have to face him sooner or later, but it had been less than an hour since Bruce had dropped her off after the trip to his parents'. *A little more time would have helped,* she thought, *but I can't just send him away. What I have to do is cruel enough without that, too.*

Watching him enter the room, Samantha made no attempt to hide her streaked makeup and reddened eyes. The moment he saw her, his carefree smile faded into a look of deep concern. "What is it, Sam? Are you all right?"

Crumpling the Kleenex she had been holding, she tossed it on the pile of other discarded tissues at the edge of the table. "Jason," she answered, "we have to talk."

Moving closer, he gazed sadly into her swollen eyes. "I'm not going to like this conversation, am I?" he asked.

"No, I'm afraid not." Her solemn reply came with great effort, and she had to look away. The hurt in his eyes was unbearable. "Bruce and I have set the date."

Jason staggered. His head lowered slowly, as one hand moved to his brow. Gradually he raised his eyes to look at her again, and in a muffled voice asked, "You're going to marry him?"

"Yes, Jason. We plan to be married next Friday."

"Oh, Sam. Is there any way I can stop you?"

Wiping her face with a fresh tissue, she forced out the words. "I'd give anything if there was a way."

"Gus could find a body for me any day now."

"Please, Jason! Don't! You told me yourself, that's never been done."

"Gus is good at doing things that have never been done."

"I'm sorry," she sobbed. "I just can't do it. I can't hang my hopes on 'maybes.' I have to face reality and get on with my life."

Jason took a couple of steps and stopped. He turned slowly and spoke some of the hardest words he had ever spoken. "You know I won't stand in your way, Sam."

"I know."

"I think you're making a mistake, though."

"Then I guess I'll have to live with it, won't I?"

"So will Gus and I."

"Oh, Jason. No guilt trips, please."

"Sorry, Sam, you're right. You deserve better than that." Walking to the mantel at the far side of the living room, he turned his attention to the picture of Bruce. "Bruce," he choked, "you'd better take good care of this lady." Without looking away from the picture, he spoke to Samantha, who was now standing directly behind him. "I once made you a promise. I said I would stay out of your life if you decided to marry this man. I never believed it would come to this, but I want you to know I will keep my word."

"Jason, I. . . "

"It's better that I go now, Sam. Better for both of us." She wanted to answer, but the words refused to leave her mouth.

When he reached the door, he stopped one last time to look back. "Would it be all right," he asked, "if I see you once more? Just to say goodbye?"

"I'll be giving up the apartment Friday morning at about ten. You could drop by then, if you like."

"I will," he said, turning to leave.

"Wait!" she cried. "The necklace you gave me. Do you want it back?"

"Would you like to keep it?"

"More than anything, I'd like to keep it."

"It's yours, Sam—and my heart goes with it."

She glanced downward and choked back a tear. When she looked again, he was gone.

Samantha spent the next week busily preparing for her marriage. Boxing up her personal things took up much of the week. She tended to keep everything, so a lifetime of memories had to be packed. She planned to store them in a spare room at Bruce's house, where she could sort them out later. She did some shopping for a few honeymoon things. She usually enjoyed shopping, but not this time. She made arrangements with the manager to vacate her apartment on Friday morning. They had planned the wedding for that afternoon.

She knew this time should have been the happiest of her life. But instead it was filled with emptiness. Even the thought of a honeymoon in Hawaii failed to excite her.

By Thursday evening, everything was as close to being in order as it would get. Bruce spent the day helping her with last-minute arrangements. By the time they finally arrived back at her apartment, it was after ten.

"I'll pick you up in the morning, darling, bright and early," Bruce said as he stepped into the hallway.

"I'd rather you didn't. I'll take a taxi."

"Why, Samantha? It's no trouble for me to. . . "

"Bruce, there's something I haven't told you."

"Let me guess. It has something to do with the ghost, am I right?"

"He's coming by in the morning for one last visit. He asked for the chance to say goodbye."

"I thought we were rid of him, once and for all."

"We will be after tomorrow morning. He's given his word."

"I don't like this one bit, Samantha."

"He saved your life, Bruce. You owe him this much."

"Oh, very well, darling," he conceded with a kiss. "I'll see you in the morning, about ten-thirty." She watched until he disappeared behind the closing doors of the old elevator.

Friday morning Samantha sat alone in her apartment, her mind reflecting on the many wonderful times she had known there. She set two packed suitcases near the door.

A lump swelled in her throat as she heard, perhaps for the last time, his voice calling from the hall. "Sam, it's me."

"You know the way in." Her voice cracked, but she managed to get the words out. She watched through watery eyes as he moved effortlessly through the closed door.

"I guess I could never get used to you doing that," she said.

"Yeah," he answered. "I guess not."

"What do you plan to do now, Jason?" she asked without getting up from the sofa.

"Well, Sam," he said, with a deep sigh, "I've already waited over twenty years. I guess another fifty or so won't matter in the big scheme of things."

She gasped in surprise. "You plan on waiting for me?"

His lip quivered as he answered. "I love you, lady. Bruce may be with you for now, but in the end, you and I will be together. It's in the contract."

"Will you be able to . . . you know?"

"Pass through the bright door?"

"Will you?"

"No. If I go through without you, our contract is nullified. I have no choice but to wait. I can't bear the thought of losing you forever."

"Where will you wait?"

"I don't know; I'll find someplace. Maybe I'll take up haunting psychologists." He walked to the sofa and looked lovingly down at her.

"I watched you grow from a child, Sam," he said with a tremble in his voice. "I saw you ride a bicycle for the first time. I was there when you got your first kiss. I witnessed your struggle through college, and I cheered loudest of all when you received your diploma. I love you, Sam. I've loved you from the first time I set eyes on you in a forest behind your grandfather's home."

Somewhere, from deep in the shadows of her memory, a childhood scene began to replay. "The army man," she said softly. "It was you."

"One thing I ask, with all my heart. Please, don't ever forget me."

"Oh, Jason," she sobbed, her cheeks warm from fresh tears, "I wish things could be different."

"You know what the hardest part will be?" he mused. "Not seeing you. At least, during the last twenty-something years, I was able to see you."

"My taxi will be here in ten minutes, Jason. I really have to go."

"I understand."

She stood and walked slowly to the door, trying to manage a smile that just wouldn't come. "Knowing you has been the best thing that ever happened to me. I give you my word, Jason—I will never forget you."

"I set you free, Sam. I wish you a long and wonderful life."

Samantha's sobs kept her from answering right away. Opening the door, she moved the suitcases into the hall, then turned one last time. "I love you, Jason." That was the first time she had ever said it. "I love you with all my heart. Please, try to be happy." She slipped into the hall. "See you in fifty or so years." The door closed, and she was gone.

* * * * *

For a long time Jason stood perfectly still, staring at the spot where he had last seen her. Alone with his thoughts and sick at heart, he sank to the sofa, burying his face in his hands.

After several minutes he took a deep breath, leaned back against the cushion, and stared, glassy-eyed, at the emptiness of the apartment. All the familiar things that were hers were gone. All that remained was the furniture belonging to the landlord. How empty and cold the place seemed without her.

Vivid memories flooded his mind. In the living room, he pictured her running the vacuum or dusting. In the kitchen she was cleaning something, or preparing a meal. Not one corner of the apartment was void of her presence.

His thoughts turned to the day, some three years ago, when she had moved in. He had never seen her happier than she was that day. She sang as she unpacked, and radiated with excitement while arranging her new home.

His best memories, though, were the most recent. It was in this very room she had learned of him, a scant four months earlier. After that came the times he had talked with her, laughed with her, and in his limited way courted her. "Oh, Sam!" he said aloud in his anguish. "I love you so dearly. How I will miss you!"

Slowly he stood and walked to the door, knowing he could no longer stay in the apartment. It was too full of yesterday's dreams. With a painful sigh, he took one last lingering look. "Goodbye,

Sam," he said. "I hope your next fifty years are filled with fun, laughter, and excitement. As for me, it will be a long, lonely wait."

CHAPTER TWENTY

With an aching heart Samantha lifted the two suitcases and crossed to the elevator, where she pressed the "down" button. In her heart, a voice kept calling out, "Turn around, go back." Giving in to the voice was no longer an option—her course was set. She moved forward numbly, unwilling to allow fleeting emotion to prolong the inevitable.

The elevator doors opened. She stepped inside, set the suitcases in the corner, then pressed the button for the first floor. The doors slid closed and the car started downward with the usual lurch. She watched the light flash, showing she had passed the sixth floor. Suddenly, the car stopped. She tried pressing the first floor button, then the other buttons, but nothing happened. The elevator would not move from where it had stopped.

She opened the cover on the little door marked "Telephone" and lifted the receiver. It was dead.

Just as the first stage of panic was about to set in, she heard a voice behind her.

"It's okay, Sam. I stopped the darn thing so we could hear ourselves talk."

"Gus!" she snapped. "I haven't got time for this! My taxi will be here any minute."

"There's nothin' ta worry about. I put time on hold. When we get through with our talk, not one second will have passed."

"If you're lying to me, Gus. . ."

"I'm not lyin'. Please, Sam, hear me out. If ya' don't like what I say, you can be on yer way to marry Bruce, like nothin' ever happened."

"We have nothing to talk about! I gave you every chance I could, and all you did was talk."

"I have somethin' for ya', Sam. Somethin' that just might change yer mind." He handed her a yellow rose.

"Gus," she said, taking the flower from him, "where did you get this?"

"I saw you lose it in a mountain stream a week ago."

"I don't understand. That can't be. How can it seem so fresh now?"

"I had it specially treated by a friend of mine so it will never lose its beauty again. That was yer wish, wasn't it?"

"How do you know that?"

"I was watchin' ya' that day. I saw when it fell ta the stream and got caught in the current. I know exactly what you were thinkin' as it disappeared in the rapids. Ya' pictured Jason being swept from you the same way. Didn't ya'?"

Samantha stared at him in disbelief. "Yes, Gus," she answered after a moment. "That's it, exactly."

"Well then, ask yerself this. If old Gus can get ya' back together with that flower, why can't he get ya' together with a certain ghost?"

She studied the rose in her hand, and smelled its lovely aroma. "All right, Gus," she conceded. "You have my attention. Make the most of it."

"First off," he began, "let me tell ya' why I waited so long gettin' around ta this little meetin'. Ya' see, Sam, there was this stipulation in the contract that required both you and Jason to say a few special words. Until ya' both said those words, I couldn't do a thing about makin' it valid."

"Special words? What special words?"

"What was the last thing ya' said to Jason, just before ya' closed the door?"

She had to think only a moment. "I told him I loved him," she answered, a tear glistening in her eye.

"There ya' have it. That's the only thing I've been waitin' for."

Opening a briefcase he had brought along, he retrieved an official-looking document and handed it to her.

"What is this?" she asked.

"It's a new contract. It replaces the old one I botched up. Don't worry, I had Maggie type this one."

"Maggie?" she repeated slowly. "Your secretary?"

"Yeah, that's right. Now, Sam, look over the contract, and see what ya' think. Oh, maybe ya' better sit down first; it could come as a shock."

She started to ask where he expected her to sit, but didn't get the words out before noticing a chair behind her. "How did you do that?" she asked in surprise.

"It's a simple thing for a talented guy like myself. Sit down."

She did sit down, and she read every word of the contract he had handed her. When she had finished reading it once, she read it again, then lowered it to her lap and stared hard at him.

"Well, Sam? What do ya' think?"

"Can you really do the things written here?"

"Just as soon as ya' sign on the dotted line."

"Be honest with me, Gus. Would I really be happier with Jason than I would with Bruce? All things being considered, I mean."

"No question about it, lady. No question at all."

She studied the contract again, even more closely than before. "Let's say I do sign this, Gus. Does it go into effect right away? No more waiting?"

"Just sign the contract and he's all yours. No more waitin'."

She didn't answer, but went over the document still another time.

Gus soon grew impatient. "What are ya' waiting for, Sam? Are ya' signin' it, or not?"

"No," she answered curtly.

"No?" he stammered. "What do ya' mean, no? Didn't ya' read what it said? You can have Jason! Isn't that what ya' wanted?"

"I'm not saying I won't sign a new contract, Gus. Just not this one. I want to negotiate a few changes in it."

"No way!" He folded his arms tightly and shook his head. "Take it or leave it, just the way it is!"

"Okay then, start up the elevator again. I have a taxi waiting."

"Now wait a minute here. . . "

"Are you going to negotiate, or do I leave? I know the trouble you're in with the higher authorities."

"That's coercion!"

"You catch on fast, for a probation officer."

"Awright, awright! We'll talk. What else is it ya' want?"

"Several things, Gus. For starters, I'm going to teach you to type."

"What!? That's the craziest thing I ever heard. I won't do it!"

"You will do it if you want me to sign the contract. I'll give you three lessons a week, until I'm satisfied you're good enough not to make another mistake like this one."

He glared at her for a long time before answering. "One lesson a week, and that's it!"

"Two lessons."

He frowned so hard, the wrinkles in his face looked like miniature Grand Canyons. "Two lessons it is," he grumbled.

"Fine," she said. "Now for the next item. You didn't mention anything in here about Bruce. I told you, he had to be taken care of. I don't want him hurt any worse than necessary."

"He's a big boy, Sam. He can take care of himself."

"Gus!"

"Okay. What do ya' want me to do about him?"

"Get him a wife. One he'll like better than me."

"I'm not going to be able to talk ya' out of this, am I?"

"It sure doesn't look like it."

"All right, then. Hang on to your hat, we're going for a ride."

"We're wha—" In mid-sentence, Samantha was swept away at lightning speed through what looked like a conduit of streaking lights. When they stopped, not more than five seconds later, she was in an office filled with computers. A lovely young woman sat typing at one of them. In one corner of the room sat a big desk with papers strewn all over it in total disarray.

"Is that your desk, Gus?" she asked as soon as she caught her breath.

"Yeah, Sam. How'd ya' know?"

"Just a lucky guess."

"Maggie," Gus said as the two women came face to face, "this is Sam. Sam, Maggie."

Maggie spoke first. "Samantha, what a pleasure to finally meet you. I've been helping Gus with your records for some time now. I can't help feeling guilty for taking the day off, you know, when the mistake occurred."

"Don't you take the blame for that, Maggie. The secretary always gets blamed for the mistakes. I know who was to blame in this case."

Maggie laughed. "Thanks," she replied. "I feel better knowing you think that way about it."

"Look, Maggie," Gus broke in, "Sam here wants to add some things to her new contract. Of course, I agree she should have that right. Could ya' help her out with it?"

"Certainly I can. Are you familiar with computers, Samantha?"

"I use the Apple at school quite often."

"If I set up my computer to the 'Apple' mode, it will work the same as the one you're used to. Would you like to amend your own contract?"

"Now hold on here," Gus objected. "This is highly irregular, lettin' a person write up their own contract. I won't stand for it!"

"Get out of the way, Gus," Maggie said, giving him a push. "You of all people shouldn't criticize someone for typing out a contract. Now, Samantha, like I was saying, would you like to do it yourself?"

"That would be great, if you can set up your computer for me."

"No problem. I'll even program it to print out on our official letterhead, with the signature blocks in place."

About two minutes later, Samantha sat down at the computer and went to work on her own contract. When she finished, she printed it out and handed it to Gus. "Maybe you had better sit down before you read this," she laughed. "It might come as a shock to you."

He looked it over. "This is highway robbery!" he snorted. "The higher authorities authorized me ta come up with the new contract, but they made it clear, it all comes out of my budget."

"Take it or leave it, just the way it is. It was your typo that caused the whole thing in the first place, and it's about time it cost you something. And—I'll bet the higher authorities would like you better if you take it."

"Maggie," he said in a gruff voice, "get on the main computer. See who ya' can come up with as a good match for Bruce. I have to get him a wife."

"I'm way ahead of you, Gus," she said, handing him a report. "I know how Samantha thinks."

"Jenice Anderson," he read aloud. "Ya' want to look this over, Sam?" he asked, handing it to her.

"Well, I'll be," she laughed. "Yes, she'll do nicely. Are you sure you can pull it off?"

"What choice do I have? At least ya' gave me a year to get them together."

"I'm all heart, Gus."

"I hardly noticed that. So, are ya' ready to sign yet?"

"Not until you sign it first."

"I thought yer grandaddy was hard to deal with. You make him look like an amateur." Gus signed the contract and returned it to Samantha.

She read his signature and started laughing. "What's so funny?" he snapped.

"Winkelbury? Your last name is Winkelbury?"

"Are you going to stand there all day pokin' fun at my name, or are ya' ready to sign the darn contract?"

"Lend me your pen, Gus. Let's get on with it."

CHAPTER TWENTY-ONE

Just as Jason was about to slip through the door leaving Samantha's apartment, Gus's voice caught his attention.

"Cheer up, fella. Things aren't as bad as they may seem."

"Oh, no!" Jason groaned. "Go away, Gus. I need to be alone right now."

"You'll be glad I'm here when ya' find out what I've been up to."

"What difference does it make what you've been up to? Sam's gone, and there's nothing you can do about it now."

"I can do most anything, when I set my mind to it."

"Yeah, like typing up a contract?"

"Okay, so I made one little mistake."

"You call that a little mistake? I'd hate to see one of your bigger ones."

"I'll give ya' that one, pal, but things are different now. My latest plan is working out great."

"You have another plan? What are you going to do, revise my contract so I'm matched up with another woman? No thanks, I'll wait my fifty years for Sam. Now go away and leave me alone!"

Jason fell back to the sofa where he lay full length, staring hard at the ceiling.

"I'm tryin' to tell ya', Jason. I got it all worked out."

"Yeah, well, if it's worked out, where's the new body you promised me? If I'd had that a week ago, I wouldn't have lost her."

"Will ya' pipe down and listen ta me?"

"I'm listening, Gus. I haven't anything better to do."

"There's something I've never told ya' about yer contract. Something that's kept me from wrappin' this up a long time ago."

"Let me guess. You made more than one typo, right?"

"Ya' really know how to hurt a guy, Jason. What I never told ya' was that one last thing had to happen before it was valid."

"You mean all these years you've let me believe in a contract that wasn't even valid?"

"It was just one little thing short."

"So, lay it on me. It couldn't be as bad as what's already hit me today."

"For any contract between a man and a woman to be valid, they have to be in love with each other. They both have to say the special words."

"Special words? What kind of game are you playing, Gus? What special words?"

"'I love ya!' Those are the special words. Until they're said, the contract won't hold water."

Jason raised his head and gave Gus an angry look. "You know I've always been in love with her. I've said your special words, time and again."

"Yeah, Jason, I know that, but Sam had never said 'em."

"She said she loved me, Gus." His voice grew soft and his words came with great effort. "In fact, that's the last thing she did say before she went off to marry Bruce."

"That's what I'm tryin' to tell ya'. The contract turned valid as soon as she said those words."

"Big deal, so now you can get me a body, no doubt? A lot of good it will do now. She's gone, Gus. She's on her way to Bruce right now!"

"Is she?"

"Yes! She is!"

"Well then, who's that standing there, right behind ya'?"

"What?" Jason whirled. He couldn't believe his eyes. "Sam!" he cried, "is it really you?"

"It's me," she said, with a huge grin.

"You came back?"

"I'm back, Jason . . . back to stay."

"Oh, Sam, I want to believe that. But if you couldn't handle it before, what makes you think you can now?"

"Gus convinced me."

"Gus? But how?"

"He made me an offer I couldn't refuse."

"An offer? What kind of offer?"

She walked to the sofa. Now it was her turn to look down at him. "I said the special words. I said I love you. That's the only thing he's been waiting for, all this time. He caught me in the elevator and explained everything."

"He caught you in the elevator? You didn't even get out of the building?"

"Oh, no!" she gasped. "That poor taxi driver. I'll bet he was furious with me."

"Samantha!" Jason pleaded, "don't leave me hanging. What happened in the elevator?"

She laughed. She had never heard him use her proper name before.

"At first, I didn't want to talk to him," she said. "I asked him to leave me alone. Then he caught my attention with this yellow rose." She held up the rose for Jason to see, and explained its significance. In finishing the story, she tried to sound as much like Gus as she could. "'If old Gus can get ya' back together with a flower, why can't old Gus get ya' together with a certain ghost?'"

"What did he mean by that? Am I finally going to get my new body?"

"Stand up, Jason."

"What?"

"I said, stand up. Now do it!" He rose and faced her.

Lifting her hand, she placed it gently to the side of his face. Then she slowly moved it up until her fingers were touching his hair. "Sam," he gasped, "I can feel. . ."

His words were never finished. They were cut off abruptly by her kiss. Gradually her arms slid around him, and his around her. Their tender embrace lasted a very long time.

Even after their lips parted, it took several seconds before Jason could speak. "Gus," he managed at length, "you got me a body. But how?"

"Well, Jase, ya' see. . ."

"No, Gus," Samantha interrupted. "Let me tell him. I'm the one who's in love with him."

"He's all yours, Sam."

She kissed him again and stroked his hair gently with her fingers. Backing away only far enough to look him in the eye, she continued. "Our contract is valid now. Nothing can ever come between us again."

"How, Sam? I don't feel any different. Do I look the same in this body as I did before?"

Moving a finger to his lips, she quieted him. "Let me finish, Jason. While we were in the elevator Gus handed me a new contract proposal, one that would replace the one altered by the typo. As soon as I read it I knew it was the answer to our problem, but I wanted a few changes in it. Of course, Gus, being the sweetheart he is, didn't argue with me." She gave Gus a big smile.

"What can I say, Sam? It's just my big streak of generosity!"

"Sure, Gus. Your generosity, plus the fact you knew it was the only way I'd sign the new contract."

"That might have had somethin' to do with it," he shrugged.

"I learned a long time ago that if you want something, you have to go after it with everything you have. The thing I wanted most was a certain ghost who's been haunting me for the last few months. But I figured Gus owed us something a little extra for the trouble his typo put us both through."

"What did you get out of him, Sam?"

"I think I did well, you know, for a schoolteacher, I mean." She grinned. "I added several things to his proposed contract, including the 'Bruce' clause."

"The 'Bruce' clause? I'm probably going to be sorry for asking, but what is the 'Bruce' clause?"

"I just couldn't bear to hurt Bruce," she sighed, "so I negotiated a wife for him."

"You did what?"

"Maggie ran it through the computer, and it came up with the perfect match for him."

"Hold on, Sam! Who is Maggie?"

"Oh, I forgot . . . you don't know about Maggie, do you? She's Gus's secretary. You'd like Maggie, she's a peach."

"You met Gus's secretary? I've known Gus over twenty years, and I've never met his secretary."

"I'm glad of that. She's cute. You might never have given me a second look if you had met her."

"No chance of that, lady! Anyway, back to Bruce. . . "

"Well, Maggie got the name of Jenice Anderson from the main computer. Jenice is Rebecca Morgan's sister. You remember Rebecca, don't you?"

"The burnt duck?"

"That's her," Samantha chuckled. "Gus had to guarantee they would be married within a year."

At that moment, the quiet of the morning was abruptly shattered by the shrill siren of an approaching rescue vehicle.

"What is that?" Jason shouted. "It sounds like it's in front of this building."

"There's been a—sort of an accident," Gus said offhandedly.

"Gus, what have you done?" Jason snapped, breaking for the window. "You've killed someone to get me a body, haven't you?!"

"Take it easy, pal. Don't go gettin' yerself uptight. All good things come with a price, ya' know."

A second siren was heard. "What price? Now there's a police car, too! What have you done, Gus?"

"I told ya', pal, there's been an accident."

"Don't play games with me! What kind of accident?"

"The elevator."

"What about the elevator?!"

"Well, Jason, it kind of fell—from just above the fifth floor."

"The elevator fell? Gus, you didn't! Did you?"

"Well the darn thing was wore out anyway. I just sorta—gave it a little push."

By this time Jason was irate, shouting in Gus's face. "Sam could have been in that elevator! She could have been killed!"

"Sit down, Jason," Gus said, using a serious voice that was rare for him.

"I don't want to sit down! Tell me what's going on here!"

During the confusion, Samantha had come up next to Jason. She took him by the arm and led him away from the window. "I think you had better sit down, Jason," she said, gently pushing him to the sofa.

He stared up at her, anticipating what she was about to say but not wanting to hear it. She smiled and held both of his hands. "I was in the elevator," she said.

"Gus," Jason said in a subdued voice. "You've killed her."

"Ya' always did have a way with words, Jason. I told ya' I was authorized ta make the deal."

"Oh, Sam! I—I'm sorry."

"Don't be ridiculous," she scolded. "What's to be sorry about? Now I'm just like you. I'm a ghost, too." She sank to his lap and slipped her arms tenderly around his neck. "Isn't this better than having me slide right through you?"

"Of course, Sam. This is wonderful, but. . . "

"But what, Jason?"

"You were killed—in a falling elevator."

"Sure beats choking on a chicken bone," she laughed. "And anyway, Gus took me out as soon as I agreed to the plan. I didn't have to go through the fall."

"You agreed to be killed? It was part of his plan?"

"It was an approved plan. I had the choice to either accept or reject it. Gus convinced me that losing a few years here would make little difference in the big picture of things. He told me I could have another fifty or so years if I wanted, but after thinking it over, I decided I couldn't be happy with Bruce. Not after knowing you. So, I made my decision."

"There's somethin' ya' should understand about her decision, Jase," Gus interrupted. "It didn't come without a price. Nothin' good ever does. It wasn't easy for her ta give up the right to live out her life. She loved her teachin' job, and she's leavin' a lot of good friends behind. She could have had the good life with old Bruce, if she wanted. She turned 'em all down for you, pal."

"You love me that much, Sam?"

She answered with a kiss.

"Are ya' gonna be all right, Jase?"

"I—I think so, Gus," he answered, staring dreamily into Samantha's eyes. "Oh, Sam," he said. "I've wanted this as long as I can remember. It's the greatest feeling I've ever had. It sure beats the way I felt half an hour ago, when I thought you were on your way to Bruce's arms."

She giggled and kissed him on the cheek. "I didn't finish telling you about the 'Bruce' clause, did I, Jason?"

"There's more?"

"Are you sure you're ready for this part? It's a little shocking."

"After what I've just been through, nothing else could shock me much."

"Okay, you asked for it. Gus has a way figured out for Bruce to meet Jenice at my funeral."

"Oh, brother! That sounds like something Gus would come up with. Although it is sort of fitting, at that."

"How so?" she asked.

"Knowing Bruce, I figure if he meets his wife at a funeral, it may be the most interesting date they'll ever have."

"Jason Hackett! You're still jealous of Bruce, aren't you?"

"I do have feelings, you know. How do you think I felt watching you kiss him? And that constant 'darling' thing drove me nuts."

"What are you fretting about? You got me in the end, didn't you? And, I have to admit, you're a lot cuter than him, even if you are a ghost."

"I'm not a ghost, and anyway he's a wimp. How do you know Jenice will go for the guy?"

"That's my problem now," Gus moaned.

"Can you do it, Gus?" Jason asked.

"Compared to you and Sam, this one's a piece of cake. Consider it history."

Samantha laid her head on Jason's shoulder and fumbled with the top button on his shirt. "Wait until you see our house," she said, in almost a purr.

"You got us a house, too?"

"Not just any house. I got us a mountain home, just like the one I was in less than a week ago. It's gorgeous."

"Don't forget, Sam. Ya' gave me six months on that one. You know, to find the right spot, and get it built, and all."

"Agreed, Gus. But if you know what's good for you, it had better have a garden and mountain stream, just like the Vincents'."

"It'll be fine, lady. Ya' got my word on it."

"You got us a house?" a bewildered Jason asked again.

Samantha poked a playful finger at his chin. "I hope you don't mind my asking for a single story. I've had it up to here climbing stairs."

This time it was Jason who kissed her. "I can't believe this is happening, Sam. I've never been so happy in my entire life."

"What a strange way to put it—for a ghost, I mean," she laughed.

"I'm not a . . . oh, what the heck." He kissed her again.

"Well," Gus said, "looks like this about wraps up another big case. As usual, I fixed up everything good in the end."

"I don't know, Gus," Jason noted. "I'd say this pretty lady had a lot to do with fixing things up. It seems to me she covered almost all the bases. About the only thing she left out was a job for me."

"Don't kid yerself, pal. She covered that, too."

"You got me a job, Sam?"

"You bet I did," she answered, tickling him in the ribs. "I plan on being a full-time homemaker, myself."

"Stop that," he pleaded, trying to catch her hands. "I can't stand to be tickled. What's this full-time homemaker thing? I thought you wanted to be a teacher."

"I'm going to volunteer to teach where I'm needed. Gus tells me I can stay as busy as I like doing that."

"I love the idea, but what kind of job did you get me? Please tell me I'm not a psychologist."

"You're a chef at the Paradise Palace. Gus assures me it's the finest. And get this—they never serve chicken there."

"A chef." Jason was glowing with excitement. "I've always dreamed of being a chef."

"You start," Samantha said, ruffling his hair, "right after the honeymoon."

"You've planned a honeymoon for us?"

"Of course I didn't plan a honeymoon. How could I? I have no idea what's over there. Maggie's making all the arrangements. I'm sure she'll fix us up just fine. After all, she is a woman. It's not like I asked Gus to do it."

Suddenly, a small flicker appeared in the corner of the room. It grew brighter and expanded until it filled one whole wall. They looked, and saw a long tunnel of light leading off into the distance.

"It's the bright door!" Jason shouted. "You see, Sam, it's just like I told you."

"This time," Gus said, "it's for you, Jason. Yer twenty-year wait is over. This one's for you too, Sam," he added. Then, with a smile and a tip of his hand, he moved into the tunnel. He appeared as a shadow before the light, and was engulfed completely as he moved away.

"Well," Samantha said, when they no longer could see him, "I guess it's our turn. Let's go see for ourselves what's on the other side of that bright light."

Jason held back momentarily. "Sam, I noticed Bruce's ring is not on your finger. Where is it?"

"It's still in the elevator," she answered. "But look! I'm wearing the necklace you gave me."

"One more question, pretty lady. I just have to know: how do my kisses compare to Bruce's?"

She smiled and kissed him again. "Bruce who?" she sighed.

"Shall we?" he asked, with a smile bigger than a new moon on a dark night.

"Yes, you crazy ghost, let's do it! Let's go home!"

Taking Samantha by the arm, Jason briskly led the way through the opening. Together, the two vanished into the light of the tunnel.

A moment later the light grew dim and was soon gone, leaving the room empty and quiet—except for the sound of the ringing telephone.

About the Author

Angels Don't Knock is Dan Yates' first novel, although he has always enjoyed working with words. "I love to express myself in writing," he says, "and would like to give church members some clean entertainment with good principles and high moral standards." He is a former bishop and high councilman, and is employed as an electrical maintenance instructor.

Dan and his wife, Shelby Jean, live in Phoenix, Arizona. They have six children and fourteen grandchildren. Dan's writing efforts have resulted in short stories in local papers and church productions. He also enjoys public speaking.